MW00872519

The House at the End of the Lane

To Leanne (Sally)
with my gratitude
Hugh Y. Rayment
Feb. 10, 2008

Hugh Y. Rayment

Order this book online at www.trafford.com/07-0735
or email orders@trafford.com

Most Trafford titles are also available at major online book retailers.

© Copyright 2007 Hugh Y. Rayment.
All rights reserved. No part of this publication may be reproduced, stored in a retrieval system, or transmitted, in any form or by any means, electronic, mechanical, photocopying, recording, or otherwise, without the written prior permission of the author.

Note for Librarians: A cataloguing record for this book is available from Library and Archives Canada at www.collectionscanada.ca/amicus/index-e.html

Printed in Victoria, BC, Canada.

ISBN: 978-1-4251-2346-8

We at Trafford believe that it is the responsibility of us all, as both individuals and corporations, to make choices that are environmentally and socially sound. You, in turn, are supporting this responsible conduct each time you purchase a Trafford book, or make use of our publishing services. To find out how you are helping, please visit www.trafford.com/responsiblepublishing.html

Our mission is to efficiently provide the world's finest, most comprehensive book publishing service, enabling every author to experience success. To find out how to publish your book, your way, and have it available worldwide, visit us online at www.trafford.com/10510

 www.trafford.com

North America & international
toll-free: 1 888 232 4444 (USA & Canada)
phone: 250 383 6864 • fax: 250 383 6804 • email: info@trafford.com

The United Kingdom & Europe
phone: +44 (0)1865 722 113 • local rate: 0845 230 9601
facsimile: +44 (0)1865 722 868 • email: info.uk@trafford.com

10 9 8 7 6 5 4 3 2

A story of love, family, and intrigue

Never a dull moment throughout the book

A book for all walks of life.
The author has relied on many experiences and obser-
vations of his own life to produce this amazing story about a
family in a growing town in central British Columbia

The names are fictitious, the places are fictitious the
events are true to life.

Hugh Y. Rayment Author

Dedication:

I dedicate this book to the people who gave me the inspiration and support as I put this story to print and especially I dedicate it to my wife Elsie who put up with the hours I spent in the computer room.

To my granddaughter Leanne Wright who posed as Sally on the back cover.

I also give my thanks to Robert [Church] Churchill who composed the pictures on the front and back covers.

To my readers who have made the decision to obtain a copy of this true-to-life story covering almost a century of Canadian living in this remote town in British Columbia, Canada.

Hugh Y. Rayment

Preface

    This is a story about a small village and its people nestled in a valley near the Monashee Mountains in the province of British Columbia. It tells about the growth of this place, I have chosen to call Carebrook, from a tiny village to a thriving city over a period of about eighty years. In the pages of this book the author has attempted to portray the many complexities of every day life. It borders on fiction and reality in an attempt to reveal everything from romance to tragedy, poverty to riches, and many other aspects of human endurance. It could be called a history book or even a study in sociology. The characters in the story, of course, are fictitious and are in no way a reflection upon anyone I know.

    Older readers will recognize the events in these pages similar to events and circumstances in their own lives. Younger readers will get a glimpse of days gone by and perhaps gain a little more knowledge of our heritage and what it is to be Canadian.

    At the age of 82 I have enjoyed putting this story to print and hope that my readers will feel the same. I think it is a good read!

Hugh Y. Rayment

Forward

"Tell us a story, tell us a story Hughie"

These words have echoed in my mind over the past 70 years or more.

They were cried out by three eager young boys when, finally, their older brothers decided to come to bed.

In his book, "The House, the Cradle of Destiny" the author describes his childhood years being brought up on a small homestead farm in east central Alberta some 80 years ago. All 5 boys slept in one large bedroom upstairs in the family home. I was one of those little boys.

After the coal-oil lamps were blown out and everyone was in bed and after much urging, Hugh would start making up stories as he went along about almost anything imaginable These stories were so interesting and true to life , and told with such fluidity that one would swear they were being read from a book. I will never forget "Chicken Little" as long as I live!

"The House at the End of the Lane" is such a story, interesting, true to life, and told in such a smooth way that the reader wants to keep on until it is finished. It is a delightful story that begins with the love of a young couple who grew up in the Okanagan Valley in British Columbia, and raised a family through the years of the great depression. As the story continues it follows the progression of the family through World War 2 , then post-war years and right up to present times. Children grew up and had families of their own and so on.

It is a story of struggle, success, failure, happiness, and sadness. It is also a great love story.

The author has an amazing memory of things that happened many years ago…to the finest detail.

This book follows on the heels of his famous book, "Camp Vernon, a Century of Canadian Military History"
With love and respect, brother Ken.

Chapter One

Little Jimmy arrived in this world on a very cold February night with the assistance of midwife, retired nurse, Mrs. Short. The birth was relatively easy because the baby was so tiny, only a little over five pounds. Sally Bette had done a thorough housecleaning that afternoon before calling for Mrs. Short. Bill Bette was not home from his job at the mill. Although his shift ended at 5:00pm he rarely went straight home. Bill was a heavy drinker and spent many of his off-hours at the local bar.

The Bettes lived in a small house at the end of the lane in a rundown part of the mill town of Carebrook. A quick glance around the house would reveal a home of neglect, very modestly furnished with what looked like used furniture. Oh, the place was tidy enough thanks to Sally who did the best she could with what was left over after satisfying her husbands drinking habit.

Bill met Sally where she worked as a waitress. She was a very attractive girl and he was a handsome man with a flare for flattery when in the presence of ladies. Their courtship was very brief and their wedding very small. He had bragged to her about the house he owned. Indeed he did own it as his father who had left it to him had passed only a few months before. He said that it needed a bit of fixing up but he would get at it as soon as they were married and said that she couldn't see it until then. Along with the house there would be new furniture and this place would do them until he could buy a new house in a better part of town. After all Bill had a good job at the mill and to Sally everything looked rosy.

The first few months of marriage were exciting enough as Sally worked her heart out scrubbing and painting to spruce the place up a bit. In the parlor there was an old chesterfield and rocking chair; heirlooms of Bill's parents. There was a well worn carpet on the floor and curtains that sorely needed replacing. A table and four chairs graced the tiny kitchen. There was a pungent odor of stale cigar smoke throughout the house. Yes indeed there was plenty of work to be done here. The bedroom was somewhat better because Bill had purchased a secondhand bed and dresser. All in all, the place had reasonable promise for an ambitious young couple starting out. At least there was no mortgage.

Sally had grown up in a neighboring village and was accustomed to a modest way of life. Her parents had a nice home and there was never any fear of wanting for food and clothing. Sally had completed high school and took the job at the café to tide her over until she found something better.

The couple were married in early spring and put off a honeymoon until they could save some money and when Bill got his annual holidays.

It was an early spring and the young couple got a start at fixing up inside the house. They got some new paint on the walls of the bedroom and the livingroom and one day Bill came home with a second hand easy chair. He made sure to announce that it was his chair. It didn't match the chesterfield and Sally let him know about it. He sloughed it off by saying,

"I'll go to the auction and see if I can get one the same color as my chair". Sally bit her lip and asked, "When do you think we can get some new stuff"? He retorted, "New stuff costs too much money."

It was about this time that Sally found out that she was pregnant and when she told Bill he retorted, "We don't need a rug rat around here." Although there had been some discord before this seemed to set off a fuse in Sally. She burst into tears and went to the bedroom and closed the door. Bill stormed out of the house, slamming the door, and headed for the bar. Sally cried herself to sleep wishing it were all a bad dream.

Bill arrived home at 3:00 am and he passed out in his chair. Sally woke to the alarm clock and saw that Bill had not slept in the bed. She ventured into the livingroom and stirred him from his sleep. "Wake up Bill! It is time to get ready for work." He groaned, stared at her and said, "Bring me some coffee." As she made him some toast the tears continued to well up in her eyes. Bill gulped down his breakfast, said "Sorry honey," and left for work without the usual goodbye kiss.

Tensions did ease up a bit for a few months and one day Sally found a bottle of booze in the clothes closet. When she quizzed him about it he said, "So what? There's a lot more where that came from." He had let the lawn go uncut for a month and stopped fixing up in the house. He frequented the bar more and more as time went on.

Sally didn't know what to do. She felt that she must make the best of it for the baby's sake. Perhaps Bill would shape up when the little one arrived. She felt too ashamed to go to her mother, perhaps fearing she might hear the words, "I told you so," because her mother and father had some reservations about Bill from the start. She thought about consulting the minister at the local Church but she was not a member of the Church and didn't think he would listen to her. Being quite new to the town she didn't have a close friend to confide in.

Sally had a relatively easy pregnancy and was able to do some improvements to the house. She managed to squeeze enough money out of the grocery budget to buy some paint and a few knick –knacks for the house. As for new clothes she had to beg her husband to even get a new winter coat. He did allow her to buy a new maternity dress and some underwear. It was with great reluctance that he allowed her buy some things for the baby. When asked about cutting the lawn he told her where the lawn mower was kept.

During the long summer months Sally took long walks down by the babbling brook and on to the small lake at the end of town. She would gaze in the water and see the little minnows swimming along, darting at a bug, seemingly without a care in the world. Oh! What a free life they had. The red-winged blackbirds perched on the rushes busily raising their young. A long-legged heron is scanning the water for a minnow or a frog. All of nature's creatures seemed to be living a life of harmony and yet she knew they all depended on others for sustenance. The only sign of conflict was when some small bird, defending its nest, took flight in pursuit of a hawk that was soaring overhead looking for prey.

One day as Sally was peering into the brook she became aware of a presence behind her. She turned around to see a young lad and his dog approaching the bank where she stood. She said, "Hello young man! What a nice looking dog you have. What is your dog's name?" "His name is Ruff and he is a good dog, friendly too. You can pet him if you like. He won't bite you." Sally patted the dog and asked the boy his name. "Tom Epston" he replied. She discovered that he lived down the block from her. She asked him if he would like to earn a little pocket money. "Would I ever," he replied. She told him that she couldn't pay very much but her lawn needed caring for. He said he would come every Saturday and do whatever she wanted him to do. This was the beginning of a long friendship and, true to his word, he was there every week and soon the place started to look much more attractive. There was a scrubby looking lilac bush at the corner of the house. It was grown over with crab grass. Tom looked at it and decided that it would be better placed near the bedroom window. He was studying horticulture in his science class at school and knew what to do. He dug it up and removed all the grass from its roots and prepared the spot where it was to go. He mixed some bonemeal and some fertilizer in with some rich black loam and planted the lilac bush in the chosen spot. With a good watering he hoped it would survive which indeed it did. It wasn't long before lush new leaves came. Sally was so excited to see it grow.

As the summer wore on Sally started to show her pregnancy. Bill seemed to be looking forward to having a son and once in a while asked Sally how she was feeling. Even though Bill spent much of his time at the bar, perhaps things were looking a bit brighter. He even allowed her to have a new stove.

He never mentioned the improvement in the yard. Tom had even fixed a part of the fence that was broken down. It must be supposed that he thought that Sally had done the work or perhaps he just didn't notice. One Sunday he was actually home and complimented Sally on how well she was keeping his house and he liked the meals she prepared too.

As the snow came and the weather got colder Tom offered to run errands for Sally. He was so fearful that she may fall on the ice and do harm to the baby. He ran to the store for her and picked up the likes of vegetables and a bit of hamburger. One day when Tom arrived at her house Sally was doing her Christmas cards and she asked him, "Tom, would you mind running down to the Post Office and pick me up some three cent stamps so I can get these in the mail." He was gone in a flash and when he returned he sat down and licked the stamps for her. Ruff lay at his feet as usual. Tom always made sure that he left before Bill got home to save any confrontation. This day, when the cards were done, he took the mail to the Post office, saving Sally that ten block walk.

Christmas was coming and Sally's parents invited them for dinner. At first Bill flatly refused to go. "Christmas is just another day," he said. "You seem willing to take the day off though," she retorted. After considerable persuasion he consented to go. It was a memorable day for Sally but her parents did not drink and in fact had none in the house. After dinner Bill became more and more irritable and suggested going home early. Sally told him to go ahead but she was staying for the evening. Finally he stomped out of the house and went to the truck and took a few large gulps from a bottle of whisky. He went for a walk and when he returned to the truck he took a few more gulps. He came back into the house and promptly fell asleep on the chesterfield. Sally's parents asked her how things were going and how Bill was treating her. She admitted that his drinking didn't make things very easy for her but hoped that he would be much better after the baby arrived.

Now it is true that Bill verbally abused Sally but he never struck or harmed her physically. He just wasn't of any help around the house. He gave Sally a portion of his pay to run the house and kept the rest for his own pleasure. When the snow came Tom came over and shoveled the walks for her. Sally often asked him to come in and warm himself and she gave him cookies and other treats that she could spare. They had long chats many times and Tom told her about his family, his school, and how he liked to play hockey. He was a happy lad and loved his mom and dad and his two sisters. Ruff was always with him and was perfectly welcome in the Bette home, at least when Bill was not there. As the time drew near for the arrival of the baby Sally found it more awkward to do her daily chores. Tom perceived this and it was not long before he was coming over after school to help her with housework. Tom sang in the choir at the Church and invited Sally to come some Sunday. She thought about it seriously but did not dare mention it to Bill. It would probably just start another huge argument so if she were to go, it would have to be on the quiet.

Chapter Two

January came and went. When the weather was not too cold and the streets were free of ice, Sally could get out and walk down to the corner store to pick up milk and bread and other little items for the kitchen. For the larger orders she had to rely on Bill to take her in the truck. One day she started to feel strange with a pressure on her back. Tom was there and she told him that she thought the baby would be here soon. She sent him to tell Mrs. Short. Tom rushed off and in ten minutes Mrs. Short was there to help with the birth. She was a wonderful lady, putting Sally to as much ease as possible. After a very short labor the baby was born.

Once Bill saw the little baby lying in the clothes basket bed he said, "My son has to have a proper cot. On my day off we are going shopping." He seemed to see his wife in a new light. He even asked Sally what they would name the baby. Sally said that she liked the name James and then asked Bill, "What would you like for his second name." Bill replied, "Of course we will have to use my second name and call him Charles. James Charles Bette, that's the ticket!" While Bill was in this fine mood Sally decided to ask him if they could have the baby Christened at the Church. Bill took a deep breath, hesitated, and said, "Sally, if that is your wish you go ahead and make the arrangements. I suppose your family will want to be there." Sally replied, "Of course they will be with us on that special day."

For a whole week Bill came straight from work and went directly to the new cot where Jimmy lay. He even held the baby in his arms and made strange noises to his son. This looked like a whole new world was opening up for Sally. Bill told her to go into town and buy a new dress and a few things for the baby. He gave her two large bank notes and announced that he had received a promotion as floor boss at the mill and every payday he would be able to give Sally a bit more money to run the house.

Little Jimmy soon gained weight and looked a picture of health. Sally provided ample milk for him and gave him all the attention a good mother could give. Tom was a frequent visitor and one day asked Sally, "How old do I have to be to baby sit for you?" "Well Tom, I think you should be at least thirteen." "Yippee!" cried Tom, "I will be thirteen in March and by that time Jimmy will be a bit older." "Yes, and in the meantime you can do a bit of practicing when you come after school." One morning, just as Sally had laid the baby in his crib there was a knock at the door. There was a lady and two little girls on the doorstep. The lady said. "Hello, I am Tom's mother, my name is Beth Epston and these are his two sisters Jane and Sue. I do hope I am not intruding. Tom has told us so much about you that we wanted to meet you." Sally invited her in for tea.

She explained to Sally that her family had lived in the area for many years. Her husband, Joe, worked with Bill and always said what a good worker he was. Sally made a pot of tea and the two ladies enjoyed a very nice chat. It turned out that Beth was a member of the Church and of course she would make all the arrangements for the baptism. Jane and Sue looked into the crib hoping the baby would wake up but he slept on. Jane asked, "Mrs. Bette, can we come down and see the baby when he is awake?" "Of course you can. He doesn't sleep all the time." As the Epstons left Sally invited them to come again. She felt that she had truly found a friend.

As time went on Bill's drinking did not stop altogether. On the odd Friday he would stop off at the bar on his way home and would finally arrive, late for supper, and a bit tipsy. Sally could tolerate this as long as he didn't go back to his old ways. As a matter of fact life was quite good and they were getting some new furniture. The house was becoming more comfortable and Bill seemed take more interest in improving the place. As it turned out, through talking to Beth, Sally gathered that Joe was a great influence on Bill's life. What a wonderful family to have met. In her mind Sally always credited Tom with saving her from a dreadful marriage; that chance meeting beside the creek.

The baby was growing and one day Sally noticed a tooth showing. This caused him to fret; sometimes waking in the night, but Sally was a very good mother and managed to settle him down so that he didn't wake Bill. Just before Jimmy's 1st birthday some spots came up on his tummy and then on his face. Jan Short came over and examined him and announced, "He has rubella, better known as the measles." Of course this is a trying time but according to Jan's instructions Sally kept him in a darkened room and kept him warm. It was a light case and Jimmy was soon his happy self again.

When the weather warmed up a bit Tom and his sisters came over and took the baby out for a walk in his stroller. It was a beautiful spring day and the birds were back, busy with building their nests and chirping loudly with their mating calls. Jimmy was fascinated when a bright butterfly lit on his sleeve.

He shrieked with glee and when it flew away a look of astonishment came to his face.

There were black clouds moving in over the lake and Sally became concerned about the children. She rushed along the path and soon came upon them having the time of their lives playing with Jimmy and making him laugh. Sally hustled them back to the house before the rain came. Just in time because the clouds opened up and a torrent of rain came down. The rain continued to fall and soon the house was surrounded in a lake of water. Because the house was in a low-lying area the water did not drain away. It kept on rising until it was leaking into the house. The rain continued for the next three days until the families in that area were forced to evacuate. Bill got as much stuff from the house as he could haul in his truck. Everything was soaked and could not be dried out until the skies cleared and the sun came out. Sally and Jimmy stayed with her mother and Bill remained in town. There was also mass flooding at the mill and had to shut down until repairs could be made. Most of the men were laid off but Bill, being a supervisor was kept on to try and get things working again. Much of the stacked sacks of grain and flour could not be salvaged. This had been the worst disaster the town had ever witnessed.

It took several weeks for the water to recede and the people could return to their homes and see what could be salvaged. The Bette family was lucky in that they had no mortgage but their property would have little resale value should they try to sell it. Fortunately they had some insurance and Sally had secretly put aside some money each month for a *rainy day.* Bill and Sally went to the bank to see what kind of a deal they could make on a new home. They could barely get enough to buy a modest home in a higher part of town. A deal was struck but it would be several months before the house would be ready. At this time Sally realized she was pregnant again and there would be additional strain on their budget.

Joe Epston was now thinking of moving to the new district but, being on a lower wage level, it wasn't quite so easy to get the financing so they would have to wait awhile. He was laid off temporarily until the mill could get back into production.

Tom's family was a little better off because their home was on higher ground and the damage was not so devastating. Tom was now moving on into high school, his voice had broken, and he was a young man. He sorely missed his visits to the Bette's but kept in touch with them. He was a good student and had his mind set on going to University to study for a career as a dentist; at least this was in his mind at the present. Often young people change their minds almost daily.

The Carebrook High School was a typical high school. The students were generally well behaved and, under the guidance of Principal John Drager, the discipline in the school was both firm and fair. The students loved his light humor and most looked forward to going to school.

As in every school, there was a clown. His name was Bolder and he was always up to something. In his welding class he was working on sort of a home made jalopy. Many days he stayed after school to work on his secret project. The rest of the students passed many remarks about it, even though they didn't really know what he was up to. Near the end of June he announced that it was ready to go. They pushed it out onto the parking lot and, after several attempts, the engine started with a belch of smoke. Bolder took it for a couple of test runs and then offered a few rides. Three passengers could be crowded into the contraption and off they went. When it came time for the girls to go for a joy ride Bolder was quite expert at handling the machine and could get about 30 miles per hour out of it. By this time the girls had been dared to give it a try. Bolder steered his vehicle onto the street and pepped up the speed. Without warning he lifted the steering wheel off and passed it to the girls in the back and shouted, "Here. Do you want to drive for awhile?" The girls shrieked in panic. Little did they know that Bolder had rigged up a couple of foot peddles by which he could control the steering. This was his big thrill of the year. He became known as "Bolder the reckless." The kids in this school were very keen on sports. They had a first class soft ball team and their football team often came out as champions in the area.

At last the basement was poured for Bill and Sally's house, Bill kept his eye on the construction as he and Sally hoped to be able to move in before Christmas. Sally took a part-time job in her father's store and her mother took on the job of baby sitter, a job she didn't mind as a temporary measure. The new baby was due in about four months so all things should work out just fine.

By November the mill finally resumed production. Most of grain crops in the area recovered after the great flood. The quality was poor in lower areas and was graded for feed. With the grain already in storage and grain harvested from higher ground there was plenty to keep the mill going. The farmland was generally good in the area and most farmers made a good living. Most had moved from horse-driven machinery to power machinery. It was at this time farm electrification was taking place and the farmers could enjoy electric light and power appliances. The greatest boon was the introduction of refrigeration. They could now store food without waste from spoilage. Roads were being improved from dirt roads to gravel and the main roads were being paved. Communications improved as well, as the telephone party lines were phased out and people could now connect countrywide. Another great improvement was the development of Rural Route mail service. Rather than each family having to go into town for their mail it was delivered to their front gates.

Some of the population was not so fortunate because the country was suffering from the "*great depression.*" The farming communities in this area however were not too badly off. At least they had food and most were employed. The mill had to keep going to provide flour for making bread and also preparing food products for the livestock. At this time Joe and Bill were fairly certain of keeping their jobs.

As time passed the Bette house was nearing completion and Sally was anxious to get moved in before Christmas. She wanted the family to be reunited again. Bill was doing a bit of carpentry work on the side so they could afford to get some new furnishings for the house. He was hardly ever seen at the bar anymore. He longed to be back with his pretty wife and of course his growing son. Jimmy was getting around now and oft times getting into the cupboards and pulling out the pots and pans. The wooden spoon through the handles put a stop to that. He was a happy little boy and of course had grandma's number when he wanted a cookie or just some time for play. Tom got out to see them on the weekends when he had time.

Tom was doing very well in school, both in the classroom and the sports field. He was looking quite athletic, broad in the shoulders, and well muscled. One Sunday he walked out for a visit and when he came in he said to Sally, "You know when I was walking along the highway, a whole string of big transport trucks passed me and I got to thinking that it would be pretty nice to own a bunch of trucks." Was he forgetting about dentistry? Of course Sally said nothing. She knew that Tom would do what was best for him. He asked Sally, "Do you think that I could go to the house at the end of the lane and take out that little lilac bush and plant it at your new house?"

She replied, "Oh, I don't see why not, but we'd better ask my husband first. Next time he is here I will ask him." Tom said that he hoped they would be able to get a house close theirs because he, his sisters and his mother missed the visits. He mentioned that there were some big machines working along the creek and he supposed they were building up some kind of a bank to protect against another flood. This would bring back the value of the properties along that street. They were also working around the mill.

As Tom walked home he felt a sudden chill in the air. He wished he had put on a heavier jacket. By the time he walked another mile the wind had risen and the snow began to fall. This was the beginning of winter and it continued to snow for three more days. It turned very cold as the little town dug itself out. The school was not far from their house so Tom and the girls didn't have to miss any classes.

One day in December Bill was told that the new house would be ready in ten days time. The excitement grew as the days ticked by. Now it was time to gather all their stuff together for the move. Sally had all her clothes as well as Jimmy's gear. Bill had his belongings at the motel and there were still items in the old house. Bill's truck would get a good workout getting all the stuff moved. Tom was right on hand to help out. The weather was very cold and the roads were icy but on moving day the sun was shining and it was a little warmer. The Bette's had to make do with the old refrigerator and stove but the washing machine, having been submerged, was unsalvageable.

When Sally came to the new house she was shocked to see a brand new washing machine that Bill had worked in with the deal. There is nothing like the smell of a new house. All the painting was done, just the color scheme Sally had chosen. The sidewalk to the house consisted of some planks laid down and they would just have to wait until spring for cement walks. The planks would be fine for now.

The move went well. It would take some time to sort things out and to put in extra shelves and things like that. Sally could look out her kitchen window and see the creek and part of the lake. The large living room window looked out on a panorama of hills, trees, and also part of the lake. They were situated not far from the shopping area. The Church was nearby and a new school was planned for next to a small park just three blocks away.

Jimmy's second birthday called for a little party at the Bette home. Grandma and grandpa, Tom and his sisters, and of course mom and dad sang a hearty *Happy Birthday*, and they all feasted on cake made by grandma. Little Jimmy took more delight in throwing the gift wrapping up in the air than playing with his gifts.

Bill was now spending a lot of time with Jimmy. He frolicked with him on the floor and just couldn't seem to wait until Jimmy could play ball with him. He would say to his son in all seriousness, "Let's go fishing this weekend". Sally was so delighted to see the change in Bill. He had turned out to be the model father. He was continually telling Sally how happy he was with his family and looked forward to an addition. He was hoping for a little girl.

Two weeks later Sally felt that strange feeling and knew

it would soon be time to give birth. This time she would not have to call on Mrs. Short because there was a new hospital in town. It accommodated only 12 beds but that was adequate for the town of Carebrook. In the wee hours of the morning she stirred Bill and told him it was time to go. They bundled into the truck and were soon at the hospital. Sally's mom had come over to stay and look after Jimmy. The baby arrived at fiveAM, a little sister for Jimmy. This time Bill was there to share the delight with Sally. Although names were discussed many times before it was now time to make a decision. This time Bill got to choose the first name and he said, "I want to call her Shelly." Sally agreed and she chose Anne for the second name. Shelly Anne Bette sounded just fine and that was the name she was baptized with.

With the new baby at home and Jimmy growing, it seemed that nothing could go wrong. The Epstons and the Bett's visited back and forth for cards and a social drink or two. This was a far cry from earlier days in Sally's marriage. Bill had another promotion to an office job and Joe moved into his position and was now able to buy a new house in the same area.

Chapter Three

In the late thirties war clouds were threatening in Europe and everybody was glued to their radios, listening to the ravings of Adolph Hitler. Veterans of the first war were particularly concerned because they knew the horrors of war and many wore the scars of the battles fought not so long ago. Neville Chamberlain's plea with Hitler and the promise of non-aggression by Hitler bore little trust with the old Vets. Finally, with the invasion of Poland and the declaration of war by Britain, reality struck home. Canadians would be, once more, going to war. Three days later, the news came over the airwaves that indeed Canada was committed to war.

The impact of this did not immediately strike home in the Bette family until one day Bill mentioned that he was of military age and he could be called into the fray. His father, now diseased, had been in the Navy during WW1 and had survived with a few close calls. He hadn't told Bill very much about it so he was thinking that the Navy would be his choice if he were to go.

Joe was quite a bit older than Bill, in his forties, and said to Bill, "You know I could wind up in the Veteran's Guard." Tom was just sixteen and surely it would all be over before he came of age. He was now in high school and some of the grade twelve boys were talking about joining up. Jobs were scarce at this time and perhaps the military would not be a bad place to be. Adventure, three meals a day, and a new wardrobe! Wow! Let me at it. Some of them went down to the recruiting station and lied about their age. The bigger ones were passed through and were soon showing off their smart uniforms and looking forward to going over seas. They also had an edge with the girls on the other boys.

Some of the younger boys joined a newly formed Air Cadet Corps. These young lads were issued with uniforms and they attended parades twice a week. They learned basic drill exercises and classroom instruction on many subjects, including aircraft recognition, basic navigation, theory of flight, aircraft construction, and, of course, discipline and military conduct rules. In the summer holidays the cadets went to camp in Chilliwack for two weeks training where they experienced life on a large Airforce base. While here they got to fly in real training planes. They learned to pack a parachute and fire a browning machine gun. They even got some time in the Link Trainer, which simulated flying in a real aircraft. The boys got a real taste of camp life. They had to parade for meals, march in squads, salute Officers, and all the other rules of the camp life. One or two of them got homesick and had to be counseled, usually by a regular Airforce Officer. At home these lads were the pride of the community. They too were popular with the girls. Many of these lads joined up as soon as they were of age.

Sally wanted no part of her Bill going to war and, in no uncertain terms, let him know about it. However, his job at the mill could be taken over by an older man or even a woman. Very soon many businesses started feeling the pinch as they lost their employees to the military. The farmers in particular felt the crunch and at harvest time one could see women out there pitching bundles into the threshing machines. As Canada started switching over to the production of war machines and materials, more and more women were donning white coveralls and taking the place of men at the machines. Large manufacturing plants were opening up across the land and one would think of it as a time of great prosperity. This was true for many but when loss of life on the battlefields was announced, it is a much different picture.

As Hitler's armies pushed across Europe the cry for more men for the forces went out. Large billboards displayed signs with a large finger pointing and the inscription, "What about you?" or "Your Country needs you now." There were pictures of men and women in uniform beckoning others to join them. Victory bonds came on the market and Canada was on a full wartime footing. Goods were rationed; particularly such items as sugar, meat, gasoline, and many items were in short supply. Manufacture of new cars was halted to make way for the manufacture of tanks, trucks, and other vehicles of war. It was very difficult to get new tires and parts for the family car. The farmers were allowed to use a special gasoline to run their farm trucks and tractors. It was purple in color and unauthorized persons caught using it by the police were fined. Some discovered means of removing the color and got away with it. Planes and ships were being turned out daily to build up against losses and to replace those lost in the air and at sea.

Canadian children were even pressed into service. Both girls and boys learned to knit scarves, socks, and mitts for the boys overseas. Many canvassed for the Red Cross. They raised money however they could to send treats overseas. Young farm boys were doing a man's work at age 13 and girls were getting part-time work to fill jobs otherwise done by adults.

As recruiting was being stepped up, Bill thought more and more about joining up. He had a feeling of guilt because he was not in the service. One day, without saying anything to Sally, he went down to see the recruiting officer who was in town at the time. It was surprising to him how quickly he got through the medical and was issued with a Navy uniform. He was given ten days to settle up affairs at home before being shipped to the coast for basic training. Now he looked pretty fine in his new uniform and he felt good as he headed for home. As he got out of his truck he suddenly became very nervous thinking about the reception he would get from Sally. As would be expected, there was a loud shriek from Sally when he opened the door. "What have you done?" she shouted. "You never said a word to me about it, and what about our children"? Bill replied, "You know we have talked about it and I just feel it is my duty to do my part. It will soon all be over and we can carry on in a peaceful country." To add to this he explained, "We all have to make sacrifices, including yourself. I will get leaves and besides, most of my pay will come home to you. It's automatic." There were some tears shed that evening but Sally realized that she would have to get used to it.

Bill had to give notice at the mill and that was another hurdle that he had to face. His boss wasn't at all happy to see him in uniform. He told him that he had great plans to expand the plant and place Bill in charge of the present one. Was this a great opportunity that Bill had missed? Suddenly the boss shrugged and said, "Well Bill I wish you the best and will welcome you back when all this mess is over." With a great load off his mind Bill set about to see to other matters. There was the question of what to do with old house at the end of the lane. At the time it was worth practically nothing. Perhaps its value would rise when the land was stabilized behind the newly constructed dike. There would probably be a demand for property when the troops started returning. Anyhow, the decision was made to hang on to it for now. As his time came to leave his friend Joe and also Tom promised to see that Sally and the children were OK. They were in good hands and Bill boarded the train for Vancouver.

At first Bill found the discipline a bit tacky but sharing it with his mates he soon fell into the routine of life at HMCS Discovery. The food was good and the training was tough. He was never a man for writing letters but soon found himself answering Sally's letters every week. The canteen was a great temptation to him but he decided to control his thirst and more and more his thoughts were about Sally. After six weeks of basic military training his group was assigned to a brand new corvette and they went to sea. They patrolled up and down the coast learning all about life onboard ship. They slept in hammocks and ate in the galley. Hammocks were used because they were suspended and compensated for the roll of the ship thus helping to prevent seasickness. Rough seas did not affect Bill much but a couple of the lads were put ashore because they just couldn't function. There was a lot to learn. Every man on board had to be fully familiar with all parts of the ship. They learned signals, gunnery, sonar, engine room operations, and even taking the wheel. Every man had to take his turn at watch. Anything sighted had to be reported to the bridge and if it was deemed to be a possible threat, "*Action Stations*", was called and each sailor had to report to his assigned station. The gun crews readied the ship's guns for action and full alert was in affect until the "*All Clear*" was announced. These maneuvers were practiced over and over again. The gun crew fired their guns at targets, perhaps a small island, and as they became proficient at that they fired at drogues towed behind aircraft. Oh Yes! These boys were well prepared before seeing real action.

Bill got his last leave before being dispatched to service in the Atlantic. The train pulled into Carebrook Station and the family was there to meet him. Joe had a car now and chauffeured the family home. Bill was astonished at how much the children had grown in his four-month's absence. Everything was in good order. The contractor had poured the sidewalks, Sally had planted some pretty flowers, and Tom had moved the lilac into its place near the bedroom window. It had even produced a few fragrant blooms a month earlier. When they drove up to the house they were welcomed by the barking of a little dog. It turned out that Tom had seen an ad in the newspaper, *"puppies for sale."* Out of his own pocket money he had purchased the puppy for Jimmy and his sister. He now had a part time job at the grocery store and had a few dollars of his own.

Everything looked ship-shape at home as Bill stepped on the train for Vancouver. It wasn't long before his ship, *HMCS Canoe* was on its way South, through the Panama Canal, and up to Halifax, Nova Scotia. This was a huge port, buzzing with activity. There were huge troop carrying vessels tied up at the wharf and, what seemed like hundreds of smaller craft lining up to leave port. The Canoe was ordered into line to take up convoy duty with the troop carriers and cargo ships out into the hostile Atlantic waters.

Chapter Four

Tom Epston, now 17 years old, and in his third year of high school, was still making top grades in his class. He was standing at his locker looking for his next assignment when he noticed a girl three lockers down from his. He hadn't seen her before and was curious. She was of medium build and very attractive with her long gold colored hair. He said to her, "Hi, I haven't seen you before. Are you new here?" She responded with a broad smile, "Yes, we just moved here from Prince George. My name is Susan, Susan Smith." He introduced himself, "I am Tom Epston and am just going to the science lab. What class are you in?" "I am just heading for my math class. I'll see you later." Tom continued on to his class with a feeling of elation. Normally he paid little attention to girls but this girl looked special. He found himself making excuses to be at his locker at the same time hoping to speak to her again. The school wasn't all that big and he was bound to run into her some time. On Friday afternoon he was walking home and saw her walking about half a block in front of him. He didn't break into a run but did speed up his pace so that he caught up to her. They exchanged greetings and he found out that she lived just two blocks further down the street from him. He didn't dare ask her for a date at this time but made up his mind that he would keep track of her.

When Tom was leaving the school he always looked for Susan and found himself waiting until she came out. This went on for a couple of weeks and one day he asked her, "How would you like to go to a show with me on Saturday night?" She replied, "That would be very nice Tom. I haven't seen a movie since we moved here." So he had done it. The date was set and he could hardly contain himself. It felt as though his heart would explode. On Saturday night Tom dressed up in his best clothes and went down the street to the Smith's house. He was a little early and Mrs. Smith answered the door. She was an attractive woman, about the same age as Sally. Tom judged. Mrs. Smith invited him in and said, "Susan will be down in a moment. Have a seat and tell me, have you lived here very long Tom?" "All my life." Tom replied. My dad works at the mill and we have just moved into our new house a couple of months ago." Susan came down dressed in a very pretty dress, her appearance leaving Tom almost speechless. Off to the movie they went with a word from Mrs. Smith, "Don't keep our Susan out too late young man."

It seems that John Smith had been transferred from the mill in Prince George and would take up his duties as maintenance manager in the local mill. He had a minor physical disability that kept him from military service. He had been hurt in a lumber mill when he was younger. He was home when Tom and Susan arrived home from the show at 10:00 PM. Susan introduced Tom and Tom said, "I am pleased to meet you Mr. Smith." Harry Smith had a stern face that broke into a smile as he looked Tom over. He walked with a slight limp as he retired to his seat by the fireside. Susan and Tom took their place on the chesterfield. As Tom looked about the well-furnished livingroom his eyes fell on a highly polished piano. He asked Susan if she could play. She replied, "My mother is the pianist in this family but I have taken lessons and can play a few pieces", Tom persuaded her to play something. She hesitated but Tom said, "Go ahead Susan. I love to hear the piano." She went to the piano and opened a songbook and started to play an old favorite. Tom stood beside her and hummed along with her and then broke into song. She was thrilled when he told her, "I sing in the Church choir on Sunday. You should come along with me and maybe you could join the choir too. They certainly could use another member." The subject was dropped and Tom soon took his leave and was headed for home.

Tom removed his snow boots and his coat and his mother with tearful eyes. She said, "Tom there has been terrible news. Sally Bette got a telegram from the military and Bill is reported missing at sea. His ship was torpedoed and sunk off the coast of Newfoundland. Some survivors have been picked but it is not known yet if one of them was Bill. You must go and see Sally as soon as you can. It is little late tonight but perhaps tomorrow after school." Tom said, "I will go directly from school and I hope she has had good news by then."

As soon as he came to the door, Sally opened it and said, "Oh Tom, I am so glad to see you. I got this telegram this afternoon and my husband is in a hospital in Saint Johns, Newfoundland. He was picked up by a fishing boat and taken to St.Johns. He is expected to be OK." It was too early to know where he would wind up. Tom's mother was overjoyed to hear the good news. She had spent the morning with Sally but had left before the latest message came.

Bill was transferred to a military hospital in Halifax where he would remain for nearly a month. Apparently his leg was injured when the torpedo struck the ship. It was not very

serious but enough to take him out of action for awhile. At the
end of April Sally got a phone call from Bill. He was on his
way home on leave. He would have to wait to see if he was able
to take another posting and return to duty on another ship.

The war news was not good in 1940. Nazi armies over-
ran the lowlands and occupied all of France. The Allied forces
had to evacuate to England in a miracle escape at Dunkerque.
Every available ship, big and small, sailed to France to bring as
many troops as possible to safety. By now Winston Churchill
was Prime Minister of Britain and his booming voice brought
hope to the people of Britain and the rest of the allied countries, including Canada. The threat of invasion of England
was real and by then thousands of Canadians were already
there. The relentless bombing of British cities and towns began. Thousands of children were evacuated from London and
other large cities. Families in the country where it was safer
took them in. As time went on, thousands were loaded onto
ships bound for Canada. One of these ships was torpedoed off
the coast of Ireland and all perished. These are the reports that
were coming to Canadian homes, stirring the blood of many.
Tom was no exception. He told Susan that he was thinking of
enlisting in answer to the call for more men.

Tom was nearing his eighteenth birthday and also his
graduation from high school. Many of his friends had already
joined up and when they came home on leave in their neat
looking uniforms he envied them. On his eighteenth birthday
he could no longer hold back. He went to Vancouver and to
the Naval-recruiting center and had his medical. He passed all
the requirements but was told there was a three-month waiting list. He was at a loss of what to do. He fell in with another
fellow who got the same story. They hung around Vancouver

for a few days. Tom found himself staring at a big sign depicting a soldier in uniform pointing his finger straight at Tom. It read, "Your Country needs you now! What are you waiting for?" Tom and his newfound buddy got on the streetcar and were soon at the gates of Little Mountain Army Barracks. They hesitated a bit and then approached a guard at the gate who quickly pointed out the recruiting office. They went through a similar medical examination as they had at the Naval Base. All OK they were whisked through the rest of the process of joining the Army. In their barrack room they got busy with sorting out all the gear they were issued with. It was all pretty confusing but, with the help of a corporal, they got it all figured out. Their first parade would be at seven hundred hours the next morning. About a week later he got a seventy-two-hour pass so he was able to go home and show himself off to his family. They were all at the station when he arrived. Of course Susan was there too. They all expected to see a young sailor get off the train but instead the beheld a handsome young soldier. All that mattered was that he was home. He was flooded with questions: "Would he be going overseas? Will you be using a rifle?" Etc, etc. There was a big surprise for him when he went to visit Sally. Bill was home on leave and would be leaving for Halifax the next morning. They all got together for a great reunion, the last for a long time. These comings and goings were very common at this time.

In the meantime the Japanese attacked Pearl Harbor and the United States was thrust into the fray. Germany had advanced into Russia and they were in North Africa. Joe had joined a militia group known as the Pacific Coast Militia Rangers. They were made up of working men, i.e. loggers, miners, farmers, laborers, or anybody who could pass the screening process. They were issued with uniforms and rifles and were given a brief bit of military training. They carried on with their normal work but, if alerted of enemy landings on the Pacific coast, they would be pressed into service. It would be like a vigilante group to fight off the invaders until regular forces could be deployed. Many of them were older men, some veterans of the Boer War and some were veterans of WW1. 10,000 men joined the force. They were all unpaid volunteers. They carried on with their regular jobs but were always ready to be pressed into service. The forest workers were natural woodsmen and knew how to tackle difficult terrain. Groups of these men were posted along the coast of British Columbia and other strategic points such as bridges, road intersections, and railroad crossings and bridges all through the interior. The Japanese launched 900 hundred bombs loaded with incendiary materials that crossed the Pacific in the jet stream, many landing and setting fires in the BC forests. The Rangers were on hand to put out the fires. Some of the balloons traveled as far east as Manitoba. When the Rangers were disbanded at the end of the Pacific War the men were congratulated for their superb job and particularly for keeping their mission a total secret so that the Japanese were never sure that the balloons ever came down in Canada. Very few Canadians knew they existed.

Susan promised to write to Tom and vowed that she was his girlfriend. Tom gave her his high school ring as a keepsake and she gave him a photo of herself, which he promised to carry with him so he could see her pretty face whenever he wanted to. She told Tom that as soon as she was able, she was going to join the Airforce. "Good Lord," said Tom, "The next thing we know little Jimmy Bette will be in uniform!" Little did he know that Sally was taking Nursing training and would soon be working in the hospital, perhaps any hospital. These were strange times indeed.

Main Street Carebrook 1920

This is main street of Carebrook circa 1920. It was taken when transportation was basically the horse. The main street was graveled but other roads were dirt and it took very little rain to change them to quagmire.

Bill Bette owned one of the first motor driven vehicles in town. It was a model T truck painted red and was the envy of the town. He used it to impress Sally or any other lady who dared to ride in it. The early vehicles used high pressure tires and it wasn't uncommon to have at least one blow-out on an average trip to Kamloops or Vernon. In later years low pressure, or balloon tires came into use along with four-wheel brakes. Gasoline was around 25 cents a gallon. These were the good old days we seniors speak of.

Chapter Five

Tom was transferred out to Camp Vernon for basic infantry training. It was here, on the parade square, that he learned his left foot from his right foot. He learned to take orders and all the other routine things a soldier must learn before his tactical training. He soon felt the comradeship of living and working with his buddies. Yes, Army life was pretty good. The food was better than some let on and there was plenty of it. It took a while to get used to lining up for the mess parades, eating out of mess tins, and washing his utensil in a large tub of water. This was a spit and polish camp and everything had to be done just right. e.g; coming on parade with grubby boots or a dirty rifle could earn him a spell of working in the kitchen, [KP], as it was called. This was a six-week course and on completion Tom would get a short leave before going on to advanced training. He and the fellow he joined up with, Len Woodal shared a double deck bed. They continued to chum around together. One day Len suggested that they should go up to the canteen to see what was going on. Of course this was a place where beer was on tap and Tom had his first taste of beer. He hadn't tried out smoking either and declined when Len offered him a cigarette. However Tom did enjoy the beer and after two or three glasses he was feeling pretty good. They decided to go down the hill into town and go to the *Dugout* where there was dancing and snacks could be bought. Tom longed for Susan so he did not stay very long.

The course wound up with a trip through the gas chamber and a final inspection by the Colonel. Tom caught the Greyhound bus home and had a wonderful time with family and friends. He spent as much time as he could with Susan and found it hard to say goodbye when it came time to leave for camp. Back in Vernon, the boys packed all their gear and marched down to the railway station and boarded the train for Calgary. On arrival they were loaded onto trucks and taken to Currie Barracks. This is where they would spend eight weeks of intensive infantry training.

Currie was situated within the city limits and a streetcar stop was right by the main entrance to the camp. The boys could be downtown in minutes. There were several dance halls where many romances got their start. Tom thought only of his girl back home so he went to places like the Calgary Zoo or the Glenmore Museum. There was also a very good pool hall in town where many of the soldiers spent leisure hours. The fact of the matter was that most of the boys were tuckered out after a hard day of training and were content to stay in camp and rest. There were camps situated in farming areas, i.e. Grand Prairie, Wetaskiwin, Camrose, and many others across the prairies. With the shortage of farm workers there was a great demand for soldiers to help out, especially at harvest time. Tom got special leave to help out at a farm north of Calgary. In spite of the fact that farm boys could get exemption from the armed forces, many of them joined up anyhow.

Tom took his training seriously, always trying for perfection. This did not go unnoticed by his training officers. One morning Tom was called off parade to be interviewed by a

Staff officer. He was offered a special course for non-commissioned officers. He was soon wearing a stripe on his sleeve as a lance corporal and giving the orders on the Parade Square. About a month later he got a second strip as full corporal and a month later he was promoted to sergeant, three stripes. Being now on staff as an instructor he got a brief leave at the end of each course. Tom really wanted to go overseas but this was not to be for some time.

With the invasion of Italy and the North African campaign in full swing, there was a need for more trained troops. Tom finally was told to report to the overseas draft company. He was given a two-week leave and off home he went. On the first night out with Susan he presented her with an engagement ring and asked her to marry him. Susan threw her arms around him and gasped, "Of course I will Tom! Can we get married right away?" Tom hesitated and replied, "Supposing I don't come back from the war. We have to think about these things." "Think about things! Tom Epston, what are you talking about?" With only two weeks things would have be done quickly and Tom said, "I will have to ask your dad you know." The happy couple wasted no time getting back to her house. Rather nervously Tom said to Susan's father, "Mr. Smith, Susan and I want to get married and I am asking for your permission." Harry Smith looked hard at Tom and replied, "My wife and I have been sort of expecting this and agree that it would be wonderful to have you as our son-in-law. Now when are you thinking of having your big day?" He replied, "Well Sir, I have only two weeks leave and then I have to report back for overseas draft."

When Susan's mom heard the news she was speechless. Finally she said to Susan, "My goodness there is a lot to be done. You will have to get a wedding dress and all that goes with it. You two will have to go directly and get a license and see the minister. Have you set the date?" Susan said, "Don't worry mom, Tom and I will get at it in the morning."

The next few days was a time of excited activity in the Smith household. There wasn't time to get invitations out but it was a small town and there would only be local guests so that the invitations could be made by phone. Special guests on the list included all of the Bette family, including Bill who had been given a medical discharge from the Navy. Susan's best friend Fran, a schoolmate would be bride's maid and Sally matron of honor. Sally's little girl, Shelly, would be the flower girl. Sally insisted on making and decorating the cake. Tom's school buddy Jack would be his best man. All seemed to be in order for the next weekend.

Joe and Beth were delighted to have a new daughter-in-law coming into the family. Joe had just returned from two weeks of military training with the Rangers, his holidays from work. His leg bothered him a bit but he assured them it would not interfere with the wedding.

The wedding morning greeted the bride with sunshine and the prospect of the up-coming event held her in a bit of a dither. Sally was with her to calm her nerves and to help her prepare for her wedding. There were no doubts in Susan's mind. She was marrying her soldier hero. The Church hall was decorated for the occasion, the cake was there, and the flowers would be delivered on time. A nervous Tom arrived at the Church well ahead of time and now all he had to do was wait for his bride. As he turned and saw her coming down the aisle on her father's arm he was breathtaken. She was the most beautiful sight his eyes had ever seen. The reception and dance after the ceremony was one happy party.

Now Tom had only two days before he had to report

back to duty; two days of married life. For the next however long he would only have Susan's picture to console him when he was feeling blue. All the arrangements were made. Susan would continue to live at home with her parents for the time being. She still wanted to join the Airforce. They made a vow to write every week and hope the war would be over soon and they could be together again. They even talked about having children. It was a sad parting at the station but Susan held back her tears and gave Tom a cheerful farewell.

Chapter Six

Tom arrived back at Currie Barracks and directly phoned Susan to tell of his safe arrival. The first order of duty was a trip to the quartermaster's stores to turn in unneeded equipment and to draw new equipment for overseas use. Each soldier was equipped with camouflage netting for the steel helmet, a gas cape, a blanket, new uniforms that were treated with anti-vermin, new boots, first aid dressings, and an emergency ration pack. On the final day they were transported to the railway station where they boarded a special troop train. Each man carried his own equipment and was responsible for it all the way. There was no checking gear in the baggage car. The seats could be folded down facing each other and three men were allotted to each double seat. They shared the space with their equipment including rifles. It was not the most comfortable arrangement but their training toughened these boys and they knew that much tougher times lay ahead.

The six-day trip across Canada was a wonderful experience. Many of the boys had not been out of their own province. The fall colors in the Maritime Provinces were spectacular. At last the train pulled through the gorge into Halifax. They were told that Chinese workers had dug out this gorge for the railway, mostly by hand. It was brutal work and they were paid only twenty-five cents a day. The train pulled up along side of the dock in Halifax Harbor. The troops were lined up in order, thirty men to a group and marched up to the gangplanks. They boarded *The Isle d'France* and were ushered to their quarters by crewmembers. All this was very strange for the troops. Many had never even see a large vessel before, let alone be on one. The ship was loaded with thousands of soldier and airmen. By the next day the ship was fully loaded and ready to start the long voyage across the Atlantic Ocean. Five days later the ship sailed into the Port of Liverpool. As the troops disembarked they were marched onto waiting trains, those funny little English trains. With a *toot, toot* they were on the move again. That evening they arrived at Camp Aldershot, a huge military base near London. There were troops from many countries, all waiting for the day they could get into battle.

Tom's group was there for only a few days before being shipped out to a training base on the seaside. Here they went through intensive invasion exercises. They were taken out on boats and when the boats came to shore the troops had to storm ashore, seeking cover from live ammunition being fired just above their heads. Clambering over rocks and through brush was not easy and of course there were some injuries. These exercises were practiced over and over again. Sometimes they had to climb up cliffs and take cover where they could find it. This was very grueling and difficult to keep up. It was not for the weak or the lazy. Most of the boys came through the course with flying colors. Sgt. Tom Epston was commended for his leadership and was later recommended for a commission.

Tom was separated from his platoon and sent off to an Officer Training Center. [OTC] This was a tough course too but not like the previous one. Here he learned about military tactics. He was given examples of difficult situations and was required to figure out the best way to get out of them with a minimum loss of life. He worked with Artillery, machine gunners, and with airforce support. Communication was a large part of the course. He learned to operate field radio and field telephone. Another part of the course was all about Officers etiquette and deportment. When he finished the course and was dressed in his lieutenant's uniform, he was a pretty smart looking man.

Tom got a short leave on completion of his course and took the train up to London. He booked into a room at Canada Place in the Officers' quarters. It took some getting used to being saluted by every non-com he met and returning the salute. Soon it became natural and he liked his new role. At the first chance he stepped into a photo studio and had his picture taken. He knew the folk' back home would be thrilled to have a copy, especially Susan.

Indeed Susan was thrilled and showed off the picture of her husband to all her friends. Sally immediately put his picture in a frame and placed it above the fireplace next to Bill's. Susan had finished her courses and thought again about joining the RCAF. When the recruiting team came to town she went to see them. They were very willing to accept her and, because of her education she could expect to get a good position after basic training. Susan was off to the coast for her basic training. She was in good physical condition and found the training quite easy. Of course it was not as severe as what the men went through.

Susan found it very easy to make friends with the other girls in her squadron. They all seemed to work for perfection in their drill and in their deportment. The girl who occupied the next bunk to her, Becky Tomm, became her best friend and, as it turned out, a life-long pal. Becky was from Oyama, a small community in the North Okanagan. She also had someone special in the Army, John Good by name. John had just arrived overseas so when they got letters they shared the news. John and Becky were not married but had promised to be true to one another while they were apart.

Sally, Susan's mother Joan, and Beth, got together weekly to compare notes and make up parcels for overseas. They also did work for the Red Cross and another organization called the Stagettes. They knitted mitts, socks, and scarves, and they cut up sheeting to make bandages for the wounded in the front line dressing stations. They also made up parcels from goodies donated by the public to send to servicemen overseas and sailors at sea. They received many letters of appreciation from the boys.

When the girls completed their basic training they were given a short leave and then shipped off to Ottawa. Susan got the job of secretary to a high ranking officer and Becky just down the hall worked in accounts. This was an ideal situation for both of them but both really wanted an overseas posting.

Tom's first posting as an officer was to a special group of Engineers. They were trained in explosives to be used in demolition of bridges, railway tracks, or any other enemy-held facility that would help them wage their war. Lieutenant Tom Epston now had a huge responsibility. He soon realized that the lives of these men were largely in his hands. They practiced their tactics over and over again until they felt they were ready for anything. With his added responsibility, Tom was again promoted, this time to Captain.

It was now 1944 and there was much anxiety with the troops as well as the civilian population. The African campaign was tidying up and allied troops were in Italy. The Russians had turned the tide and were driving the Germans back. It was they who cried for a second front in Europe. Allied forces were built up all were ready for action. At last on the morning of June sixth thousands of ships streamed across the English Channel. The Coast of France had been under bombardment for forty-eight hours. The troops stormed ashore and the invasion was on. This memorable day, known as D-day would see allied forces penetrating the German lines in a solid bridge-head. Tom's crew of ten men had sped across the Channel in a speedboat and came ashore unscathed amongst all the confusion. In his briefing Tom had been told that his first objective was two concrete gun emplacements, [bunkers]. They scrambled across the beach and over some rocky ground and right up to the bunkers. They were below the gun openings and threw their deadly charges home. That was the end of two guns and their crews. Tom noted that two of his crew had been hit on the beach but the rest came through without a scratch. As they moved on they came across a suspicious looking steel plate. They called out, "Surrender!" They saw the plate being moved aside and twenty stunned looking German soldiers emerged with their hands above their heads. Tom, with two of his men escorted the prisoners back to the beach. A crew had been put ashore to put up a barbwire enclosure and there were already about two hundred prisoners under guard there. Tom noted that they were standing there with a look of disbelief that such a mighty army could be defeated. Of course the battle was far from over and there would be thousands of casualties on both sides before it was all over. Tom awaited further orders before rejoining his comrades. The two that fell on the beach were both killed and those dreaded telegrams would be sent to their families' back home. The dead soldiers, allied and German, were placed in temporary graves with their i.d.'s attached and would later be transferred to official war cemeteries. Where possible a padre would perform a short burial service. Each soldier was wrapped in his issue blanket for burial.

It was about a week before Tom got the chance to write a note home. The shelling was almost constant and preservation of life came first. However he got a brief respite from the front when he was called back for a briefing and orders. Headquarters was in a house and he actually got to sit at a table and write his first letter home. He couldn't divulge anything about his location or what he was doing but he was able to tell Susan that he was OK and that he loved her and to give his regards to everybody there. He now had to address his letters to Sgt. Susan Epston.

When Tom got back to his men one of them was missing. He asked, "Where is Dusty?" One of the men replied, "He caught a bit of shrapnel but he'll be OK. We took him to the first aid post and they patched him up and then sent him on to the 1st Canadian Field Hospital." Another piped up and said, "I think he will be back with us. It didn't look very serious." Capt. Epston told the men that he heard that they were unloading mail at the staging area and there may be some parcels from home. "We have to go back to headquarters anyhow so we will start back after dark. There was a hell of a battle up near Caen and it is reported that there are a few Jerries hiding out near here." It was relatively quiet where they were at the present but they could see the flashes and hear a constant blasting of the big guns. Occasionally there was the rattle of a German machine gun quite close by. Tom and his men laid low until after sundown. The air was filled with a mixture of gunsmoke and smoke from burning buildings. Also in the mix there was the pungent odor of rotting flesh. The weather was hot and the bodies soldiers, German and Canadian, still waiting for the burial party. There were also the bodies of hundreds of farm animals that got in the mix. The only reprieve from this stench was with a heavy rainfall.

Tom and his little party, now seven, started their treck back to headquarters, keeping as quiet as possible. An ambush was a distinct possibility. They arrived safely and were able to bed down in a hay shed. They awoke in the morning to the thundering sound of exploding bombs. Caen was getting another going over by allied bombers. Tom showed the men where to get cleaned up and get some food in their bellies. He came back to them with new orders. He needed two men and the others would join another group. He said, "This is a pretty risky job and I want you to decide who will come with me." It is not known how they made their decision but Lefty and his buddy Wayne volunteered. The job was indeed risky. The little party was issued with wet suits and flippers, watertight pouches for explosive materials and their weapons. They also carried snorkels and emergency rations for three days.

Tom laid out the plans for the assignment. They were to enter the River Laison and move upstream to a bridge and destroy it. They would be in enemy held territory so would have to move at nighttime and lay low in daylight hours. The bridge was about two miles from the start point. They bid their buddies' farewell and trudged toward the riverbank. The water was murky, probably from all the shelling and bombing. After the first big bend in the river they knew they were in enemy territory and they couldn't dare show themselves. The water was fairly warm at this time of year so that was not a problem. As soon as it was dark they set out in single file, about twenty yards apart. They moved slowly forward, using their flippers and snorkels. When the bridge came into view dawn was not far away. Tom directed them to a place where reeds would hide them. They decided to stay there and observe until nightfall. As daylight came they could see that there were two guards posted on the bridge and there was considerable amount of German military traffic moving toward the front. This was a very strategic bridge. Not only was it a supply route but, in case the enemy had to retreat this would be a main escape route.

As soon as it was dark the men moved up under the bridge. They had to attach the explosive exactly to insure that the bridge would come down. The problem was the guards. Another obstacle was that a searchlight swept the bridge every half-hour. The guards didn't seem very vigilant. Lefty said, "Come on Wayne let's do them in." Tom stood by with his handgun drawn and the two boys started their climb up the girders of the bridge. To help them out both guards were smoking and leaning on the far side railing. They were busy in conversation when they should have been patrolling the deck. Just after the next sweep of the searchlight Lefty and Wayne rolled over the railing and cut the throats of the two guards. Back in the water the three men hastily planted the explosives and drifted back to the patch of reeds, trailing the detonator wires with them. Tom said, "Let's wait until the next convoy comes and then we will let her go." They didn't have to wait very long and three panzer tanks rolled up onto the bridge. Tom pressed the button and everything went sky-high. The bridge deck was in the river along with the tanks.

The searchlight came on and German troops were swarming to the site. Tom cautioned the men to submerge, lie perfectly still, and just expose the opening of the snorkel. The Germans were scouring the banks of the river, at times only a few yards from Tom and his boys lay. They didn't dare to move and lay there until about an hour before dawn. The whole show had been an enormous success but now to get back to their own lines.

At 400hours they decided to take the chance. Again they spread out in formation and put those flippers to work. At one spot they could hear dogs and German language. The boys just froze where they were until they could no longer hear the dogs. Then, in frenzy, they moved along as fast as they could. The current helped them along and just as daylight broke they were home free. They were given a big welcome back and after a hearty meal of stewed bully beef they lay down for a well-earned rest.

This heroic fete was rewarded by a mention in dispatches for all three of them. Some time later on the Canadian Press got hold of the story and it was written up in the hometown paper. It was only then that Susan realized the true dangers of war and the peril that Tom was in.

The boys got a ten-day rest at headquarters before their next assignment. The gunfire could still be heard but at least they weren't in constant contact with the enemy as the front line boys were.

However they were always within range of enemy guns and bombing from the air. Fortunately the German airforce was pretty well knocked out of existence.

Meanwhile, back in Ottawa, Susan was very concerned about Tom's well being. She rushed to the mail office every day to see if there was a letter from Tom. He had explained to her the difficulty of getting the opportunity to write. The one thing she dreaded was the thought of getting a message from the Department of National Defense. Her friends told her, "No news is good news." One day Susan was called to Squadron Leader Simm's office. She said, "I have been looking over applications for overseas service and came across yours. How serious are you about going over there?" Susan replied, "Well, Ma'am I feel sort of useless here when my husband is over there in all that danger. Maybe he could get a leave and we could get together." Squadron Leader Simms told her that there were some postings and she would see what she could do. "You know that your job here is very important and you are doing an excellent job. Actually I have been considering you for a commission. It may be a good idea for you to go to O.T. C. before going over there because there is little possibility of promotion there." Susan thanked her and returned to her desk.

True to the Major's word, Susan was selected to go for her officer's training in Kingston. Her only regret was having to leave her pal from Oyama. Oh well! This is the Air force!! Her training went well and she graduated with top marks. She was now, Lieutenant Epston and proud to wear a pip on her shoulder strap. Susan got a leave and went back home to Clearbrook. Everybody was so proud of her. They all compared notes they had received from Tom and others who had gone off to serve their country.

Susan went to visit Joe and Beth. They too, were very concerned about Tom's safety but all they could do was pray that he would come out of it in one piece. Joe talked about his Job as a Ranger and in confidence told her, "I know I can tell you and it will go no further. We were called out a couple of weeks ago because a strange object was seen in the sky. It came down in a wooded area and exploded, setting fire to the brush. The fire was quickly extinguished and we were sent in to investigate what had caused it. In the explosion there was not much left of the object but we were able figure it out. The Japanese were launching balloons loaded with incendiary material into the jet stream, which carried them across the Pacific to North America. Some have been reported as far east as Manitoba. The purpose was to set fire to valuable timber stands and field crops. We mustn't let word leak back to them that they are doing damage or where they are landing." It was apparent that the war was coming home to Canada. There were also ships being torpedoed in the St Lawrence River as far up as Quebec City.

Canada was on a full-scale war footing. Rationing of certain goods was tightened up and some were just not available. New domestic appliances were just not being manufactured. The John Inglis Company in Toronto was now making guns rather than washing machines.

When Susan reported back to Ottawa she found that Becky had taken over her desk. To her delight Susan was on the next draft to England. She would be in charge of a new group charged with documenting casualties as they were being sent back to Canada because of wounds or illnesses sustained in the service of their country.

The war was now extended to Northern Belgium and into Holland. Tom now had a different job. He had been promoted to the rank of Major and was in charge of a special assault team. Although it was a very precarious job, he remained in headquarters and away from close combat. On occasion a few shells came to stir up his adrenaline but they were in a pretty substantial dugout they had taken over from the Germans. Canadian troops had crossed the Leopold Canal successfully after a terrible effort by the Algonquin Regiment. They were now battling the Bresken's Pocket and up to the Scheldt Estuary. This was a particularly brutal part of the war because much of the land had been flooded. The dikes had been blown, letting the seawater in. It rained almost constantly making life miserable for the troops. Slit trenches filled with water as soon as they were dug. Casualties were mounting daily from both wounds and deaths. Many were evacuated because of illness or complete exhaustion. This was known as the battle of the dikes.

One morning the sky was filled with aircraft. This was the fatal day of the Arnhem parachute drop. Tom looked up at the mass of gliders and troop carrying aircraft. Surely this would be the drive to end the war. Through some serious miscalculations and bad luck the raid that was to trap the bulk of the German Army failed miserably. This would extend the war through the winter of 1944-45.

Becky got a surprise one morning when she opened a memo that was left on her desk. She was to report to the office of the Secret Service. Now what on earth could they want with her? She reported at 900 hours as directed and was ushered into an inner office marked Private. She was seated in front of two male officers who proceeded to interview her. They had all her Military records in front of them. First they went over each document for her approval and the senior officer,

Squadron Leader Macdonald, spoke up and said, "Miss Simms, you have an enviable record and we are looking for someone with good staying power as well as a very good memory. This is a top-secret assignment that would require you to work shifts around the clock. Have you had any experience with radio?" Becky replied, "The only thing I know about radio is how to turn it on and find the station I want to listen to." The Colonel said, "That is a good start. We will train you. You will have to learn a number of enemy codes as well as our own. In your course you will get training in several languages used in those codes. Behind this office is a very high security room equipped with short-wave radios and the operators have to listen in a number of radio bands and record any messages going back and forth between military commands." Becky answered, "I would like to give it a try Sir and you can count on me to keep all secrets. Who will I be reporting to and when can I start?" "You will report to me or the Wing Commander here every day unless it seems to be of an urgent nature and then you will report directly to this office. Your assignment will start immediately, that is tomorrow. I expect you have things to clear up in your present job. You will start by pairing up with other operators and there will be daily instruction periods. You will work only day shift until you feel competent enough to go it on your own." "I am very anxious to get started Sir and thank you for selecting me." As Becky left the office the Wing Commander said, "By the way, there will be a promotion for you as soon as all the paper work is done."

Becky was one happy young lady. She couldn't wait to write home to her folks but could only tell them that she was on a special assignment and not a word about the nature of it. From now on all her personal mail would be censored as it was for any other members of the forces who were on active service.

Now this was indeed an interesting job. She kept the headphones on during her shift and recorded any messages she could pick up. It was all in code but she soon began to recognize what was meant. One message she intercepted was from one U-boat to another and when it was deciphered it turned out to be a plan to torpedo a ship in the mouth of the St. Lawrence. She took it to the Colonel immediately. A Canadian destroyer was immediately dispatched and both U-boats were destroyed before they could let their deadly torpedoes go. Becky's group was also able to pick up dispatches from Japanese planes and ships. Becky was now a Sergeant and was very proud to show off her three stripes when she got leave. The war wore on into winter and the hopes of an early victory seemed to be dashed. In fact the German Armies mounted a huge offensive know as the Battle of the Bulge. The American forces were routed and there was a threat of cutting off all of the Canadian forces in Belgium and Northwest Holland. The Germans were counting on reaching a huge American fuel supply facility before their fuel supply ran out in their tanks and other vehicles. Fortunately the Americans foresaw the threat and they destroyed the fuel. The Germans did in fact run out of fuel and were forced to abandon much of their equipment. The bulge was pinched off by the British and Canadian forces and, once again the war turned in favor of the Allied Forces. The Russian forces were forging ahead, the Germans were driven out of Italy, and the Canadian forces were moved up into Holland. Eventually the Rhine River was crossed and now the war progressed in to the German Heartland. There was still some heavy fighting to come as the Germans reinforced their lines with fanatic Hitler Youth and SS troops. They were prepared to fight to the finish; they even shot their own soldiers that attempted to surrender.

Tom's group was now involved in seeking out strongholds and destroying them. These were concrete bunkers manned by suicidal troops who literally did fight to the finish.

Tom's former buddy Lefty was again wounded during a daring raid on a German machinegun emplacement and spent a month recuperating. On his return to active duty he was assigned to an infantry unit now operating in Holland. The going was tough. Much of the land was flooded and the rain came down day after day. One day Lefty got a letter from his girlfriend back in Canada. She told him that she had met a very nice fellow who worked in the same factory as she did. He had asked her to marry him and she had accepted his proposal. The rest of the letter was an attempt at an apology. This was known in the Army as a "Dear John letter." Lefty was heart broken of course and he pretty much went to pieces. His sergeant noticed his plight and got him a few days back at headquarters to settle down. There was no way he could get leave to go home and try to do anything about it. This was not an uncommon occurrence and, in some cases, it was the other way around. In the months waiting in England the troops met pretty English girls and romances resulted in girls back home getting similar letters. Some married men didn't even bother to inform their wives of their romantic encounters and some just stopped writing home period.

There were many unplanned pregnancies on both sides of the ocean. One fellow met a Dutch girl and they had two children out of wedlock. He planned to marry her but got shipped home before that could be arranged. He wanted to bring her and the children to Canada but immigration would be difficult unless they were married. With some influential help in Holland they managed to arrange a marriage by proxy and indeed they did come to Canada and had a real wedding. There were cases where an illegitimate child grew up in his/her own country and years later took measures to immigrate to Canada and seek out their fathers. In some situations a great deal of embarrassment resulted.

In Britain the optimism rose and they saw there was a chance that peace was near at hand and that families could be brought together again. Susan was kept very busy in her job, always hoping that Tom's name would not appear on her casualty lists. Would he still be the same man she married so long ago? As long as his letters kept coming she knew that he would be. As for Susan herself, she had survived the dreadful V-1 and V-2 bombings that had terrified the people of Britain and on the continent throughout the past five months of the war. The V-1 was a huge bomb with a motor attached. It was launched from a ramp and directed toward certain target areas, e.g. London. It flew across the English Channel with just enough fuel to reach its target. When the fuel ran out the engine would stop and the bomb would come down. It was a terrorizing weapon because nobody could tell where it would land and when it did it, the devastation was terrible. The V-2, on the other hand, was a rocket. It was fired from a pad and traveled at super-sonic speed so that there was no way of knowing when or where it would land. The saying was, "If you hear it, you have survived." These two weapons, called Hitler's secret weapons, were devastating to humans and structures alike. As the launching facilities were over-run by the allied armies, this menace ceased to be a problem. By April Hitler's Empire was crumbling and the end was in sight. Berlin had been all but obliterated by around the clock bombing. It was reported that Hitler and his lover Eva Braun, after a hurried wedding, commit suicide in a bunker in Berlin. German command was passed on to Admiral Karl Donnitz of the U-boat division of the German Navy. He was the official who signed the unconditional surrender of all German forces, ending WW2..

After the surrender there were still pockets of fanatics who continued to offer resistance. Some of these fell under the responsibility of Major Tom Epston. His crew was sent into these places and made every effort to get them to surrender without a fight. In most cases they were successful. On the 12th of May, Tom was taking his crew into a small wooded area where some rifle fire had been reported. Through loud speakers they conveyed the message that the war was over and that surrender would guarantee safe passage into the custody of the Canadian Army. Just as they approached the wood a shot rang out and a bullet shattered the windshield of Tom's Jeep.

A piece of glass made a small slash in the side of Tom's cheek. There was a lot of blood but the wound was not very serious. The boys scattered into the woods and soon brought out a half dozen prisoners. These Germans hadn't received orders to stop fighting. Tom's wound was soon patched up at a field dressing station and that was the last action of his unit in WW2.

Chapter Seven

Now it was on to peace-keeping duties for Major Tom Epston. He was placed in command of a unit in Duisburg, a German city not far from the Dutch border. This became a major point for processing German prisoners and getting them back to their homes. Those who were members of the Gestapo, SS, or Hitler Youth were transferred to another camp for further screening and interrogation, etc. Many of the returning soldiers found very little left of their homes to return to as they had been destroyed by the massive bombing and shelling of the cities. Not as many of the farm homes were destroyed because they were not considered to be military targets. Where the Germans used these buildings as strong points they were destroyed by artillery fire or burned as the allied armies moved into Germany.

This posting only lasted for three months and then Tom took command of a repatriation center for Canadians located not far from London. Susan was stationed a twenty minute bus ride from there. At last they were together in some sort of permanence. Tom managed to arrange the use of a staff car and they were able to rent a small flat in the village near Susan's camp. Here they were able to bide out the time until they got on the draft for home. They also got to travel around the country and see the people getting back to a normal way of life. It was a wonderful sight to see the towns and cities lighted up at night after five years of blackouts and darkness.

After another six months Susan and Tom managed to get on the same ship headed for home. It was the Queen Mary and she would dock in New York.

Although the ship was loaded with troops, war brides, and children, the trip was much less stressful than when they went over the first time because there was no fear of U-boats or enemy ships or planes. It was not long before they were sailing past the Statue of Liberty into New York Harbor. What a beautiful sight to welcome them to America. A few days later they stepped off the train in hometown Carebrook.

Susan and Tom arrived home just in time for the official homecoming for all the Veterans in the district. It was to be held two days hence. The morning dawned with a glorious sunrise. The Veterans, all decked out in uniform, formed up in front of Town Hall. From there they marched down Main Street led by the School band. Never had there ever been such a large crowd gathered in this quiet town. Everybody was out to cheer for their heroes. The parade proceeded down to the auditorium where a feast, prepared by the ladies of the parish, was laid out for them. There were speeches and toasts to welcome the Veterans home. A special plaque with the names of each Veteran along with the name and crest of the unit in which he/she served was presented to the Mayor. Another plaque with the names of those who did not return was also presented. These plaques were later mounted in the foyer of Town Hall in an official ceremony.

Tom recognized most of the returned Veterans and there were many happy reunions as they enjoyed a drink or two at the bar. John Good, Becky's husband, was there. He had arrived home a month before Tom and he had married Becky and had settled down in a small apartment at the south end of town. There was shortage of housing at this time and Tom was on the search. They could stay with his folks for the time being but really wanted a place of their own.

One weekend Tom and Susan were over visiting Bill and Sally, enjoying a game of cards. Of course the subject of housing came up and Bill said, "You know Tom, I still own that little house at the end of the lane. I know the house isn't worth very much but since the land was built up the property would be suitable for building a new house." That House had a certain amount of sentimental intrigue for Tom and he asked, "What would you be asking for it?" Bill thought about it for a moment and then said, "Tom, I will have to think it over and I will let you know in a couple of days."

That evening Bill and Sally talked it over and, because Sally always had a soft spot in her heart for Tom, she said, "Oh Bill, It would be so nice if we could give them a break." Bill was back at the mill working full time and in a management position so was able to give Tom a good deal. He decided to give Tom and Susan the property and they would not have to start paying for it until the new house was built and they were moved in. This was a huge help for them. Besides that the property was just large enough for them to apply for benefits from the Department of Veteran's Affairs. The only thing was that Tom had to have a job. Tom had always been interested in horticulture but he would require more schooling to get a permanent job. Upon inquiring at the DVA office in Penticton he found out that he could get aid to help him to continue his education. Susan found no trouble getting a job in her father's store and as both were Veterans they were able to get money for the property and Tom could attend University in Vancouver. It would mean another separation for a few years but in the end they would have a new home and Tom would have a good income.

They met with Bill Bette a few days later and a deal was struck. Sally was thrilled that they could help out. All the arrangements were made. Susan would stay with her parents at least until Tom got settled in University and she was certain that she could get work at the Coast. Tom got registered at UBC, ready to start the Fall Semester. There was emergency housing for Veterans at the Little Mountain Army Camp. This would work out just fine for all concerned.

For John Good things were not so easy. When he got home he felt disoriented and had no confidence in the future. His army experience had not been a happy one. He had trouble adapting to taking orders Army style and did not always obey orders and consequently spent time in the guard house, On one occasion he was given 30 days detention. Although Becky was true to him while he was away she was a little dismayed at the boy that came back. They dated a couple of times but John seemed distant and unreceptive to her eagerness to carry on a renewed relationship.

Susan met Becky for coffee one afternoon and John's behavior came into the conversation. Susan suggested that perhaps a bit more time would heal him. It wasn't that John had been exposed to front line action; it was just that he hated the Army. Perhaps he would buck up when he found a job and got back into a normal routine. Susan would talk to Tom's dad and see if there was something at the mill for John.

John's condition seemed to get worse and finally Becky pleaded with him to go to the doctor. Following a thorough examination John was referred to Shaugnessy Hospital in Vancouver where John was diagnosed with a large tumor on his brain. He would have to undergo immediate surgery. When she heard this Becky caught the next train and took a room at a nearby hotel. It was a long operation and John barely survived. When Becky arrived at his bedside in the recovery room he did not show any signs of recognizing her. The surgeon spoke to her and said, "I am sorry to say that it may be a long recovery period." John had sunk into a coma that, in itself, was not uncommon and he would probably come out of it within the next day or two.

The days passed and John remained in the coma. Becky had to get back home and was not much good her staying anyhow. She would have to wait to hear from the hospital and pray that it wouldn't be much longer. She phoned the hospital every day but the answer was always the same, "No sign of movement yet." Becky stayed with Susan for the time being but Susan was going to be moving to Vancouver to be with Tom.

One morning, in the third month, Becky was doing some ironing when Susan called to her and screamed out, "Come to the phone, there is news from the hospital." Surely enough John had opened his eyes and stared around the room. Becky had never packed her suitcase as fast in her life and was down to the train station. When she saw John he looked at her strangely and didn't seem to know who she was. The nurse told her that it would take time. As he recovered Becky was there every day and when he was able to get up she wheeled him out in his wheelchair. One day he said to her, "you know nurse. I think I know you from somewhere." Becky replied, "Of course you do John. You even asked me to marry you before you went over to fight in the war." John stared at her and smiled a big wide smile and said, "You know Becky I don't think that is a bad idea." "Are you proposing to me again?" she asked. That was it and she accepted in a quivering voice with tears of joy welling up in her eyes. At last her dreams would be answered.

Little did Becky know how long John's recovery period would take? Would he be able to hold a job and would she have the stamina to look after him for years to come? These were the questions in her mind but one thing she did know was that she loved him and wanted to have the chance to help him out and perhaps give him some children.

Bill still owned the house at the end of the lane and was hanging on to it until Tom finished his university courses. Bill and Sally were chatting about it one evening after supper and Sally mentioned that Tom and Susan were coming home for the Thanksgiving weekend. "Good!" said Bill. "I will find out where he wants to locate their new house, possibly he can give me some drawings, and I could start dismantling the old house." Sally said, "For goodness sake, do you think you can handle that on top of your work at the mill?" "Well," he replied, "I have two years to do it and perhaps Becky's husband could give me some help." Bill had grown to respect Tom as his own son and somehow wished that Tom and Susan would provide him with a grandchild.

When Tom and Susan arrived they were immediately invited to stay with the Bett's. They had a big enough house to accommodate six couples for the Thanksgiving dinner. Sally was delighted and the three ladies got together to prepare the feast. When Susan took her coat off it was quite evident that Bill's wish would soon come true.

She was pregnant and kept it as a surprise for this occasion. After dinner they were sitting before the fireplace enjoying a sip of brandy when the doorbell rang and in walked Becky and John. He had just been released from hospital and came in without the aid of a wheelchair. This was indeed a time for celebration. "Just think of it,"

Joe said, "I will be a grandpa." "This was certainly a time for celebration and thanksgiving too." said Sally. They all lifted their glasses to toast the day.

Bill and Tom got together the next day to talk about the property deal. They agreed on the location of the house but Tom felt that it would be too much work for Bill. However, taking a stab at it could do no harm. As for house plans, he and Susan would work on that. Bill said, "Well, for sure you have to have a nice room for my little pal when he comes". Tom's mind went back to when he first knew Bill and thought, "What a change and indeed what a grandfather image to have for their little one and others that may follow?"

As soon as he got the chance Bill was down at the old house at the end of the lane, planning how to take it down. He felt quite sentimental about it now remembering the days of his childhood there. He recalled playing along the banks of the creek and bathing in the lake. It was getting cold by now; otherwise he might have stripped off and gone in for a dip. The garden was overgrown with weeds. It needed Tom's loving care and would soon have it. Now Bill didn't believe in wasting anything and started taking walls down inside and saving what lumber could be salvaged. It was good solid wood and had been well preserved over the years. He was able to store quite a bit of it in the old shed and perhaps some of it could be used in the new structure. Bill only worked on it for about an hour after work and then on Saturday afternoons. He made sure to be on hand to help Sally with grocery shopping and running errands. They were a loving couple and Bill often commented on her beautiful blonde hair and blue eyes.

Bill often took his son Jimmy with him to work on the house. He was surprised at how much the young lad could do.

He helped with piling the boards in the shed and even spent some time removing the old nails. Jimmy was a good boy and always wanted to be with his father. Sally was delighted to see them working together. Bill taught him many skills that would serve him well throughout his life. Bill was a good worker himself and expected the same of those who worked with him. He was well liked at the mill and was respected by the new workers that trained under him. At Christmas time the families all got together. They attended Church services, even Bill, and did all the traditional feasting and celebrating. By now John was much stronger and Joe got him a job in maintenance at the mill. He was overjoyed when Bill asked him if he would like to help out at the house. On Christmas morning Becky announced that she and John were tying the knot in April. It would be a spring day when all the life is returning to the forests and the fruit trees would be coming into bloom.

John turned out to be a very willing worker at the mill and while he helped Bill at the house. By mid-March the house had been completely dismantled and the salvaged lumber neatly piled and protected with tarps. All that remained to be done in preparation for the new building was leveling and excavating for the foundation. Bill had a friend with a bulldozer and it wasn't long before all was set to start laying the foundation. This work would have to wait until Tom came back with the plans.

The date for the wedding had been set for April 15th so there was a flurry of activity to get ready for the big day. Weddings in this town were major events that seemed to involve everybody. This one was no exception. Tom and Susan would be home at semester's end. Their baby would be arriving shortly after the wedding. John and Becky managed to find a small apartment that would do for the time being. Housing was in short supply and they decided that the small suite would be better than moving in with family.

Tom and Susan brought with them plans for their dream home. It would be a three-bedroom bungalow with a fireplace and a large covered deck. The property was large enough for a good sized garden and some fruit trees. They were so excited as they went over the plans with Bill. There was a reliable contractor in town and he agreed to start on the house the following month. Sally had persuaded Bill not to get involved in the building but he could keep an eye on its progress.

By the time they had all the approved permits from the town planners it was near the end of September. The excavator came in to dig out the basement and prepare for the footings. Once this was done the crew came in to put in the forms for the foundation and the basement walls. Next came the cement crew with the mixer, wheel barrows, levelers, and other tools for making a smooth job. In these times the cement was mixed on site and poured into the forms from the wheel barrows. It was back-breaking work but these men were used to it. After a few days the forms could be removed and construction could begin. Weeping tile was laid around the foundation to insure good drainage and a dry basement. The outside got a good coating of tar to make it waterproof. The plumbers had laid the sewer pipes and the water line before the basement floor was poured. This was one of the first houses to have underground wiring so that there were no unsightly power poles on the property.

Now the carpenters moved in to start construction of the rest of the building. Every part of it, including the roof trusses, were cut and assembled on site. Prefabrication was not yet in use. Power saws were in their infancy and much of the work was done with the handsaw. These men were true craftsmen and they showed great pride in their work. The basic structure was made from fir that was well cured. They were able to use some of the wood from the old house but in most cases it was more trouble preparing it than it was worth. Every stud and every board was nailed securely in place. At this time the outer siding was shiplap and tar paper and stucco wire was installed in preparation for the scratch coat of stucco.

By now it was well into November and the contractor was anxious to get the roof on and shingles laid before the snow came. The windows were ordered and on site in good time so the men could get them installed, closing in the building. Inside could be done in the next three months. The natural gas line would not be coming through there for a few more years so they would put in a propane heating system. This could be converted to natural gas at a later date.

At this stage the wiring and plumbing was roughed in. All the waste lines were of cast iron and caulked together with molten lead. Plastic coated wiring was just being produced. All splices had to be soldered and taped. All receptacles were mounted in metal boxes. All the building codes had to be adhered to.

The rage at this time was to have coved ceilings and sand finish plaster in the interior walls. Stippled ceilings were a fairly recent innovation. In preparation for the plaster, building paper was nailed to the studs and wooden slats were nailed into place, leaving a small space between them to secure the plaster. A scratch coat of plaster was applied in preparation for the finish coat. All this was time consuming work but by the Christmas break all that was left to do was the finishing work including painting and installation of lighting and plumbing fixtures. The house would be completed by the end of the University year in April.

Tom and Susan came home for the Christmas holidays and were thrilled at the progress of their future home. Susan had the greatest time picking out the paint colors for the house. Tom was more interested in how they could utilize the basement and where he planned to build a garage. The old shed would have to be removed at some time but in the meantime it could be used for storage. There was much to celebrate that Christmas. Susan's baby was due in February and she opted to come home for the event. She would stay with her folks until Tom finished school. At that time they could think about occupying their new home. Bill was as excited as anybody. One would think that the new baby would be his own grandchild.

Around this time there was a bit of labor unrest in the Province and many workplaces were affected. The mill had to lay off help because the Teamsters went on strike and product couldn't be moved out. Bill and Joe were not affected because they were in management but John was not there yet. He was laid off temporarily. This was a hard blow because he and Becky were just getting on their feet and were looking for a house to buy. With the growing baby the suite was a bit crowded and the last thing they needed was a stoppage of pay. These people pretty much stuck together and it wasn't long before Becky was working in the store with Susan's father. Luckily the strike lasted only a month and they were back to work again.

Susan arrived home at the end of January to have her baby. She got settled in with her mom and waited for her time. On Feb.10th she felt rather strange and wanted to go over to the new house to wash the floors. This is often referred to as the nesting instinct. Of course her mother wouldn't allow her to go. Surely enough, about 3:00 am Susan woke her mother and said, "I think it is time to go" There was a scurry of activity as they got her hospital stuff into the car and they were off to the hospital. Susan was a few days past her due date and the doctor told her it would be a very large baby. The labor pains were very severe and they carried on till morning and through most of the day. At 5 o'clock things started to happen. Her mother was there but in those days nobody but the doctor and nursing staff were allowed in the delivery room during a birth. Finally the baby arrived. It was a boy and Tom was phoned immediately. There was a loud shout of joy heard when he got the news. Tom didn't often show much emotion but this was the exception. He admitted later that he had celebrated into the wee hours of the morning. He only had two more exams to write and he would be on that train in a flash. They named the baby Thomas Joseph Epston. Sally's two children were approaching their teens and it wouldn't be long before they would be starting middle school. Bill spent a lot of his spare time with his kids. He said he couldn't wait until he could watch Jimmy play on the school hockey team. Shelly was an image of her mother. She had the same blond hair and blue eyes as Sally. Of course Sally kept her prettied up and made pretty dresses for her. Shelly was delighted with bright colors and shrieked with joy when she got new clothes. Jimmy was more like his father; a rather serious boy but was very obedient and easy to raise. Soon after Tom got home he rushed over to the Bette's to see the children and, of course, his old friend Sally. She was still very special to him. The lilac he planted beneath her bedroom window was just bursting into bloom.

Now Tom got the chance to practice his horticulture. The house was finished but the land was a mess. The old garden was overgrown with weeds and grass. It would take more than a shovel to get this into shape. The best way to handle it was to get a machine in to clear away brush and till the soil.

Ten loads of good black loam had to be hauled in to level off the low spots. When it was all leveled off he got some rolls of lawn grass and had an instant lawn. He wanted to plant some fruit trees and a couple of red maples for shade. As the men were loading up the waste Tom noticed a sprig of green. He recognized the shape of the leaves and salvaged the plant. It was the remains of the lilac bush he had moved to Sally's house. Tom planted it by the bedroom of his own house and so the tradition carried on. Susan got to pick out the flowers and shrubs she wanted around the house and by the walkway. After a couple of weeks of hard work the place was beautiful. Everything now appeared to be ready for them to move in. They got their things together and, with the help of family, they were in .All that was needed was a few pieces of furniture and the house at the end of the lane was one of the best looking houses in town. Tom had another year of studies at UBC but Susan and the baby would be very comfortable while he was away. Her friends and family would see to it that she had help any time she wanted it.

There was one important thing to be done before Tom went away. The baby had to be Christened. This was another huge gathering and the Church was filled. Baby Tom wore the same christening gown that his father had worn. Beth kept it safely and it was now the traditional gown for any new babies that were to come to this family for years to come.

Chapter Eight

On the north-east corner of the lake there was an Indian settlement [reservation] covering a whole township of land. They lived in shacks with no electricity, water, or sanitary sewerage disposal. They lived in deplorable conditions by Carebrook standards. They were treaty Indians and derived their living from fishing, hunting and a little bit of farming. They came into town every Saturday with sacks of fish to sell at the market. The hardware store handled their furs. There is little doubt that the prices paid for their goods were very meager. The women made very colorful garments from hides they tanned themselves. They were decorated with colored beads purchased from the general store. These items were very popular as gift items and visitors to the town bought the slippers and other items of clothing made by these women.

Alcohol was a problem with the Indians, both men and women. At this time they were not allowed in the beer parlors so they turned to making their own liquor in the form of wine or moonshine. They were more susceptical to getting drunk and getting into trouble with the law. Some of the concoctions they brewed up were dangerously poisonous to their systems. Largely they were ignored so long as they didn't come into town and cause a disturbance. In spite of this they were generally law abiding people. They had their own school, taught by white teachers. Very few went past grades four or five so that any of the young girls seeking jobs in the white community could only get menial jobs, such as dish washers or housemaids or work in the local laundry. Some of the men got construction jobs.

There came a time when the government decided that the Indian children should have a better education. The children were rounded up by the authorities and sent to residential schools run by Catholic and Protestant Churches. Many of them were there against the parents wishes and of course the children were under terrible duress being separated from their parents. The schools were very rigid in discipline and their dormitories had a lot to be desired. The children were terrified of their teachers and were threatened not to tell anybody of their treatment there. There were several people who realized the conditions on the reservation were appalling and tried to find a remedy but there really wasn't much that could be done. Driving by the reservation one could see two or three wrecks of cars sitting outside the shacks. What was the reason for this? The answer is simple. An Indian could not get credit at a bank so had to pay cash for anything he wanted to buy. The car dealers were not very sympathetic and when a car was traded in it might have a cracked engine block or some other major defects. They were dubbed as Indian cars. When an Indian came in to buy a car he could probably get one of these cars for about $100.00. It would do well to get as far as the reservation. There was no come back so he just had to wait until he saved up another hundred bucks and try another one.

The Indians were great horsemen and some of them entered in the bronco riding and other competitions at the local rodeos. Some were lucky and won a bit of money. Most of it was spent on booze but a few of them bought good saddles and riding gear and even got to ride in national competitions such as the Calgary stampede. The Falkland rodeo was another event that attracted riders from the reservations. A good source of cash was from raising rodeo horses and selling them to the rodeo circuit.

As time went on the government, through the Department of Indian Affairs, started building cheap houses on the reservations and conditions did improve. Children were taken from the residential schools and schools were established on the reservations. This was a great relief to the parents and children alike. At this time Indians did not have a vote in elections and therefore considered to be second-class citizens. No treaty rights had been signed and land claim issues were coming to light. This was to become a very serious issue. A few of the native men were going on to higher education and some became lawyers and stepped into some of the affairs of dealing with the government on native issues. The process was very slow, offering to take years for any resolutions. There were definitely some improvements taking place on the reservation.

Bill Brown had bought some more land and increased his cattle herd. With it the work load increased. He had bought a couple of horses from Joe Drake, a member of the Indian band. Joe was a hard working man who ran a good operation and seemed to have a good head for business. Bill hired his son Jerry to work on the farm with Gary. The two of them got along very well with little supervision from Bill.

Gary took on the position of foreman and made very good decisions to the benefit of the, now called, ranch. Another member of the band, George Downs had a fine herd of cattle and he also was a good manager. He wanted to get some machinery and do a bit of grain farming on the reservation. Of course he could not get financing to buy the machinery and the dealer offered no credit. When Bill heard

of this he went into town and talked to the bank manager. The manager would not budge on their policy of no credit to Indians. Bill explained to him that this man was a sound business man and he could be relied upon to pay back the loan. After a few strong words the manager said, "Well Bill, if you are willing to back him I suppose I could put through a loan for $2,000.00." Bill replied, "Your damn right I will and there are a couple of others out there I would do the same for. Most of them are good people if only they were given a fair chance." Bill left the bank feeling as though he had done his good deed for the day. The next morning he drove out to Georges place and gave him the good news. George went with Bill and they signed the papers at the bank and then on to the machinery dealership. He was able get a good used John Deere tractor, a plough, a disk, and a used seed drill. This would give him a good start now that spring was near. He had to clear a bit of land which went much easier with the tractor to pull roots. He sold the logs to the lumber mill and was able to buy some seed grain with the proceeds. This was the break he needed and he went on to run a profitable farm.

When Joe Drake got to hear about it he became very interested and wanted a similar deal. Of course Bill could only stretch his own credit so far and Joe would have to wait another year. He had heard that raising buffalo would work well on reserve land. An area would have to be fenced with a sturdy six foot fence and there had to be access to water. It was decided to make it a band operation but the thing was to get financial aid from the government. Once again Bill Brown went to work for them. He had to get some letters of reference from the business people of the town and then lobby the Department of Indian Affairs to get a grant for such a project. It took three years before a herd of twelve buffalo arrived at the reserve. Now all of the members of the band had access to a good supply of meat. They shared the responsibility of looking after the herd. As they progressed there were less and less problems with alcohol and crime. This was a prime example of what could be done through co-operation between both communities and Bill Brown could take credit for getting the ball rolling. There was another issue that took years to resolve. The Indian lads who had joined the Army for both WW1 and WW2 were not granted veteran's benefits when they got home. They just went back to the reservations and made out the best they could. This was one of the factors that lead to very heavy drinking. These boys were super soldiers, some winning battle honors for bravery. This was a very sore spot in Canadian history.

The men of the Merchant Navy suffered a similar treatment by the government. They were not classified as veterans and yet their wartime service was every bit as perilous as any of the fighting men. As a matter of fact the men of the Merchant Navy were at war and in danger every day for the five years. Thousands of them perished at sea, victims of enemy action.

The government's point of view was that these men received higher pay than the regular forces and therefore were not eligible for any government compensation.

In most cases Veterans were guaranteed that they would get their pre-war job back when they returned home. In one recorded case a merchant seaman returned to his old job but later when an army veteran returned the seaman was bumped and the army veteran got the job. It is certain that many like events occurred.

As Tom settled into civilian life he had some trouble

sleeping at night. He often cried out as he experienced flash backs of his war experiences. He was told by his doctor that it would pass. Over the next ten years these dreams did not abate. He contacted Veterans Affairs but they offered no solution. They also told him that it was caused by his war experience and that time was the only cure. This worried Susan and she was forever coaxing him to seek specialists to see if there were something that could be done. Nobody seemed to have an answer.

It was not until after the Viet Naam War that American Doctors gave it a name; post traumatic stress disorder.[ptsd] They pointed out many symptoms for it and recommended psychiatric treatment. It was not recognized by Veterans Affairs until Peace Keeping Forces were returning suffering from the trauma of seeing mass death scenes in places like Bosnia. A couple of fellows at the Legion visited a psychologist and took several treatments. These two fellow set up sessions at the Legion and they invited other veterans to attend. Most veterans were reluctant to attend or even talk about it because, in their minds, they saw it as a weakness. However those that did attend got great relief from it. It seems that those suffering from PTSD need to get together and talk about it in a private environment. Everything is brought out, including the terrible experiences that caused the affliction. One chap stuttered terribly and after a few sessions his stuttering almost ceased to exist. Once a person can cast aside the thought that he is the only one afflicted and he can share it with others, he is well on the way to relief from this terrible affliction. It was not long after this that PTSD was recognized as a pensionable disorder.

Chapter Nine

Everything seemed to be working out to be the best for the people of Carebrook and in particular our featured families. It appeared that all the men had secure jobs. Tom went for an interview with the personnel manager of the forestry department and had been offered a position as soon as he graduated from UBC. It wasn't exactly what he wanted but would be a well paying job until he could go into research. This was now his aim.

Bill found his job at the mill to be quite stressful because he was now in charge of all personnel, the safety program, and the general running of the operation. The owner of the mill was getting on in years and showed up less and less at the office. He felt that Bill was very competent and that he would take over as general manager within the next year or two

One morning, just before noon, Sally saw Bill's car pull into the driveway and Joe was driving it. He told Sally that he had just taken Bill to the hospital because he had a very bad pain in his chest. Sally cried, "Please take me there right away. I will call Susan to see if she can come over and look after the kids." In a few minutes Susan was there and Joe and Sally headed for the hospital. Bill was in emergency and looked very frail lying on the gurney. The doctor was with him checking him out. He told Sally he wanted to speak to her in the office. Bill was wheeled away into another cubical and Sally went to the office to see Dr. Watson. "What is wrong with him?" she asked. The Doctor replied, "It is a little early to say until some tests are done but we suspect that it might be pneumonia. With no complications he should be out of here in about ten days." Penicillin was now in common use and should make short work of the infection.

Sally went to his bedside and stayed with him until the nurse came to take him to X-ray. Bill found it very difficult to speak but managed to tell Sally not to worry. Susan came to pick her up and comforted Sally as they drove home. Sally said, "Bill has never had more than a cold since we were married and he is healthy as a horse so I expect he will throw this off pretty fast." Susan offered to stay with her overnight and that she would do anything she could to help. Tom was away at the time so Susan and her youngster took the spare bedroom.

The next morning Sally waited for the phone to ring and bring some good news. Finally Dr. Watson phoned and told Sally that it was more than what he had suspected the day before and suggested that she come in to his office. She hurried off to the office and was ushered into Dr Watson's office. He said, "Mrs. Bette, I don't want you to be too alarmed but your husband has a suspicious looking shaded area on his left lung. It may be just some fluid there but we are doing more tests and we will know in a couple of days."

"What other possibilities are there Doctor Watson?" "There are two possibilities Sally. It could be tuberculosis or, in the worst scenario it could be a malignant growth. We will very soon have a positive diagnosis. He will get the best possible care here in Carebrook but he may have to be moved to Vancouver." Sally was obviously shaken by the news but made up her mind there and then that she would be brave and stand by him no matter what.

The following two days were days of hope and prayer. Bill's condition remained the same. He was given pain killers that allowed him to sleep but while he was awake there was some pain. On the third morning Sally was called to come to see the doctor. As she sat in his office waiting for him she had a feeling of dread and despair. When Dr. Watson came in he said, "Sally, there is no easy way to tell you what we have found. Bill has extensive evidence of cancer. At best the left lung will have to be removed and we can only hope that the cancer has not spread to other parts of his body. The surgery will have to be done at Shaugnessy Hospital in Vancouver. He will get the best of care there under direction of one of the best surgeons in the country." Naturally Sally was shaken by the news and asked the doctor. "Is there a place where I can stay close by because I want to be at his side as much as possible?" "Indeed there is. There are rooms right on the premises especially for that purpose. I will see to it that you get one, and please don't hesitate to ask me or those who are treating Bill any questions you may have." He added, "Keep your chin up and I suggest that you pay a visit to your pastor for spiritual help. There is a lot of power in prayer."

Sally left the doctor's office with a heavy heart but as she walked down the hall to Bill's room she made up her mind to keep up a cheerful front while she was with him. Doctor Watson had already told Bill what had been discovered and that he would be moved to the Coast. He told Sally not to worry too much. He was a pretty tough guy and would beat it somehow.

As soon as Tom got the news he phoned Sally and told her he would be there for her. "Any help you may need please call on us. We can look after the children for you while you are away." Jimmy and Shelly loved going to visit Auntie Susan and Uncle Tom. [This is what they called them] The arrangements were made and Sally and Bill were on their way by ambulance.

When the operation got under way it became quite evident that the cancer was much further advanced than first diagnosed and the most they could do was extend his life for a few more months. This was tragic news but a fact that had to be faced. As soon as it was possible Bill was transferred back to Carebrook where he would be near family and friends. He was never to see the home he loved so much again. The doctors kept him on pain killers as much as possible. Sally spent every hour she could spare at his bedside. A month later Bill passed away in his sleep. The whole town mourned his passing and he was given full military honors at his funeral. The Legion members were out in full force and supplied a color party and bugler as they bid farewell to their comrade, Bill Bette.

With assistance from Veteran's Affairs Sally was able to carry on at the house and raise her children on her own. She would work part-time and of course her family and friends would keep an eye on her. Tom would look after her plants and her garden and do any repairs needed around the house. Both children would soon be in high school and there was a reliable neighbor who offered to watch out for them when Sally was not there. Sally mourned for many months at the loss of her dear husband but managed to cope and get on with life. She had the two children that occupied much of her time and in the long evenings she did a lot of reading.

One day Sally came across an ad in the paper that offered lessons in painting as a hobby. She thought about it for a few days and decided to look into it. The instructor was an accomplished local artist and it turned out that she was also a widow about the same age as Sally. Her name was Margaret

Croft and some of her work was on display in art galleries in Vancouver and Victoria. Sally got the necessary supplies and was soon attending classes and practicing what she learned at home. The house had a small den which she shaped up as a studio. This was a whole new world for her and it wasn't long before she discovered a new talent she never suspected was in her. One day Shelly got into her oil paints and made a bit of a mess on one of her paintings, [trying to improve on it]. This prompted Sally to have Tom install a lock on the door for her.

Joe and Beth were frequent visitors as well as her mom and dad. As always Tom and Susan came over for cards and often had Sally and the kids over for dinner after Church. Once a month they all took in a movie and went out for dinner at a local restaurant. Tom and Susan were members of the Legion and invited Sally to go there with them for an evening out. There was a lively band playing and they had a great time. There were other forms of entertainment there and Tom thought she might like to become a member. This would take a lot of persuasion because she didn't feel ready to expand her social life at this time.

Jimmy and Shelly were both doing well in school and seemed to be growing up too fast. They were turning the radio up a bit too high for Sally's tolerance and she was for ever telling them to turn it down. They often came home with the latest hits on records and stereo was now the rage. Sally bought a new stereo for the family room in the basement with the proviso that the kids keep the volume at a reasonable level. Sally allowed them to have friends in and often they had a pizza party and she was always included for the feast. Both of her children were pretty well behaved and good scholars. They had good habits with regard to homework and Sally always took great interest in their school activities and their achievements. Shelly was in the drama class and was forever practicing for some play or other. Jimmy had his shop class and came home with various pieces of work he had put together. Metalwork was his favorite and one day he asked Sally for some money because there was something he wanted to make for the house and he had to pay for the material. To her surprise he came home in a truck. A buddy's father had picked up Jimmy's work of art at school and brought it home. It was a yard light post with an address arm on it. Tom came over and installed it in the front yard and ran an underground wire to the house. It was an enviable addition to the Bette home. Tom always saw to it that Sally's front lawn and flower beds were kept neat and well groomed.

For the children a new craze had started. Every child had to have a *hoola hoop*. This was a plastic hoop about 3 feet in diameter and the child placed it around his/her waist and moved the body so that the hoop swung around, staying in position at the waist. This was mostly a girl's thing. Bicycles were very popular for boys and they often got together and had races. In many communities safety conscious parents formed peddle – pusher clubs. Volunteers taught youngsters safety and care of their bicycles. At the end of the course the kids decorated their bikes and held a very colorful parade down the main street of town. There were riding skill competitions with prizes and each child who passed the course got a graduation certificate. This program was fully supported by the whole community and the Police Detachment as well. Carebrook bragged that all its children from ages 7 to 14 took this training.

Tom's position with forestry was a good one and covered the surrounding area. He spent many hours in the forest but at least he was home every night. His little one was now walking and learning to talk. One night Susan said, "You know Tom, it is about time we had a playmate for Tommy. Tom said, "You know Susan, I have been thinking about that too. I want a little girl around the house." "Well", Susan said, "You won't have to wait too long because I am already two months pregnant. I saw the doctor this morning and he confirmed it." They clicked their glasses of wine in celebration of the coming event and now all they had to do was wait to find out if it would be a boy or a girl. Both agreed that it didn't really matter.

The next couple of years were relatively uneventful. The children were growing up. Jimmy's voice had broken and Shelly was nearing teenage and was Miss Popularity at school. She had taken the leading role in a number of school plays. Oh Yes! Susan gave birth to a little girl she named Grace Elizabeth. Tom was ecstatic. He had his little girl. They loved their house at the end of the lane. It seemed that it would always keep this name as it was known by all the townsfolk. Joe and Beth were the proud grandparents and were frequent visitors. John and Becky now had two children and had moved into a nice house not very far from Sally. On occasion all of these people got together for a picnic or a night out at a club house by the lake. It had been built as a community project and families or groups could rent it for special occasions. Joe was president of the organization and Susan was secretary treasurer. They tried to improve on it each year. The latest project was to winterize it so that it could be used year round. It was ideal for groups of up to 30 people.

Carebrook was generally a peaceful place requiring only a small detachment of four constables at the Police Station. They were occasionally called out to the local beer parlor to break up a fight or remove somebody who was getting a bit too rowdy. There were no parking meters. There was the odd fender bender but there were no records of serious crime. It was a very nice place for people to live and raise their children.

One morning the town woke to the shocking news that, Jane Foster, one of the girls from the high school was reported missing and there was a call for volunteers to form a search party. This young girl; only sixteen, was a top student and popular with all her classmates. She often visited with her friends for an evening and then walked home.

She was always home by 10:30 and her parents didn't worry about her. On this particular occasion she wasn't home at midnight nor had she phoned to say that she would be late. Her friends said that she had left for home shortly after ten. The route home was down near the lake and was fairly well lit with street lamps. People in the area were asked if they had seen or heard anything suspicious. Tom and Susan had come home from Sally's about that time didn't notice anything out of the ordinary.

Under the direction of the Police, the search got underway, concentrating in the area along the lake. No trace could be found of Jane and the search area spread to cover all parts of the town and the nearby forest. Police dogs were brought in from Vancouver to help in the search. Three days went by without a trace of the girl and her parents were in a state of desperation.

One of the neighbors came back from a trip to Prince George and was shocked to hear of the missing girl. He had left for Prince George on the night that Jane disappeared. He said that he recalled seeing a red pick-up stop momentarily on that road as he was backing out of his driveway. It was headed west and that was all he saw. This was the first break in the case and an APB was sent out across the country to be on the lookout for a red truck with a young girl as a passenger. With no license number it would be hard make a case of it.

A few days later another break came. A red truck was found abandoned on a forestry road twelve miles from town. It had two flat tires and there was evidence that it had been driven on one flat tire for nearly a mile. An intense search was set up in the area and, although there was a dread of what might be found, there was a feeling of hope that they were on the right track. Every inch of the forest was searched but nothing was found. The police were busy checking ownership of the truck and found it was from Kamloops. The owner had not been seen for a couple of weeks. At least they now had a lead in the case and it shouldn't take very long to find out where the owner was hanging out.

Upon investigation it was found that the truck was registered to a Jack Stipe. He had a brief criminal record for break and entry but wasn't considered to be much of a threat. In the investigation some threads that seemed to match the color of the coat that Jane was wearing were found on the seat of the truck. Jane's parents were certain that she would never accept a ride from a stranger and they had never heard of the name Stipe. There was only one set of footprints leading from the truck. Jane had either been dropped off at an earlier site or she had been bodily carried from the truck by the culprit.

A break finally came in when a logger reported a body near where he was working. It indeed turned out to be Jane's body. She had been brutally assaulted and strangled. A hundred yards from there another brutal sight was discovered. Apparently Jack Stipe had hung himself from a tree. As one observer said, "At least it saves the cost of a long court case."

The whole town grieved for this beautiful girl and everybody attended her funeral. This was the first recorded murder in the history of Carebrook. The sorrow-stricken family placed a notice of thanks to all who had taken part in the search and for the hundreds of flowers that had been given in sympathy. This gave some sense of closure to a very sad event in this small town in the interior of British Columbia.

Chapter Ten

Jimmy and Shelly were growing up and as ever the pride and joy to Sally Bette. Their report cards from school showed average grades. Each had their own specialty. Jimmy loved working with metal and thought he would like to be a welder. In his instructor's remarks it was mentioned that Jimmy had a special artistic flare in his work, Jimmy is a good student, and he has the qualities of a good tradesman. These are the kind of remarks that can make any parent proud.

Shelly still excelled in drama. She was able to put expression and poise into her acting. Her voice was clear and loud enough for all to hear. For that reason she usually got the lead role in many of the productions put on in the drama classes. Would she someday be a movie star?

Sally continued with her painting and was turning out some very nice pictures of British Columbia scenery. One day she tried to include a picture of a bald headed eagle gliding over a lake. She tried and tried but it didn't seem to look natural enough. Her instructor spent hours with her and told her not to try and put so much detail in the feathers. After all in the distance the detail would not show anyhow. Finally she got it to look real. Mrs. Croft told her that perhaps if she wanted to do detail she should try her hand at close up paintings of birds. Here is where her talent lay. With a bit of practice she did some paintings that were good enough to enter in the local art show. To her surprise she got second in her class. This encouraged her to expand her talent to painting wild animals and very soon her paintings took on a new life.

At the spring art show she presented three pictures. It was the largest show in the valley at that time and there were artists from all over the interior and a couple from Vancouver. One of the artists, a middle aged man, kept coming back and looking at one of Sally's paintings. Finally he asked her if he could buy it. The price tag read $250.00 and he gladly paid it. This was her first real sale of any consequence and she felt very proud and perhaps a little important. Of course she was and she deserved every bit of it. The gentleman who bought the painting introduced himself as David Frost. He was a handsome man with a touch of grey at his temples and a small moustache. After the show David came to Sally's table and asked her if she would like to join him for a bite at a nearby café. She accepted the invitation and off they went. Sally and David talked about their art experiences and their successes and failures at various art shows where their work was exhibited. David explained, "I got my start in the art class in high school in Penticton. I had a very good art teacher who encouraged me to go on and improve my talent." He had been married and had a teen-age son Bill. His wife had been killed in a tragic car accident on highway 97 just a year ago. David had been very successful and had sold many paintings; mostly wild life and landscape in both oils and watercolor. He was now collecting paintings from British Columbia artists. He said that he saw something very striking in Sally's work. She told him of the tragedy of losing Bill to cancer and how she had buried her sorrow in her art work.

Before saying goodnight they agreed to meet for lunch on the next Saturday at the same café. David lived on an acreage beside the lake about two miles from town. He called it his sanctuary; a quiet place where he could commune with nature and practice his painting. Bill took the bus to school and spent his spare time studying books on aviation. He wanted to go on to college and take up aero-engineering. David was a quiet man, tall, and quite handsome. He drove a sporty car and dressed in fashionable cloths; casual but attractive. Sally and he made a fine looking couple. Sally had no mind for romance at this time but did enjoy being with David and exchanging ideas about their art. Their first "date" at the café was very casual and they enjoyed a good chat. Neither discussed their financial status. It was obvious that they both loved wild life and relaxed conversation to go with their art work.

Sally's youngsters, now into high school were lively young teenagers and seemed to have insatiable amount of energy. They both were doing well at school and caused Sally very little anxiety. They were good kids. One day Sally saw Jimmy carrying books for a pretty looking girl as he walked her home a couple of blocks past her place. Jimmy told his mom that he liked Peggy a lot and was taking her to a show on Saturday night. This was his first date and he took plenty of time to spruce himself up for the occasion. Sally told him to bring her home and introduce her. He said, "Yes mom, in due time." Peggy Jackson was indeed a pretty girl with long blonde hair and blue eyes. She was a member of the school band and wanted to take up the harp. Her music teacher played the harp and was thrilled to have a student who wanted to follow in her footsteps. She offered special lessons in the evenings and Peggy signed on.

Shelly took on ballet lessons to improve her balance for

her dancing lessons. She was a very happy girl and it was a delight to hear her laughter as she frolicked around the house. Sally had to check her up about keeping her room tidy and also for talking too long on the telephone. These traits were all part of growing up. Sally's parents adored their grandchildren and often made excuses to drop in for a visit. They were also pleased to know that Sally had found a companion to share time with.

Tom and Susan were frequent visitors at Sally's house and they loved to play cards. One day she invited them over and said "I have a surprise for you. I have invited my friend David over and maybe we can make it a foursome and play partners." This was a grand idea. Tom and Susan instantly liked David and asked him if he played bridge. Neither Sally nor he had very much experience in that game but were willing to give it a try. Tom had played it quite a bit at the Officers' Club and volunteered to help the others learn the fundamentals of the game. This became a weekly pastime for the two couples over the winter months.

As time went on the little sports car was seen more and more in Sally's driveway. There was still no talk of romance between them but it was obvious that they cared a great deal for each other. They gave each other a peck on parting but not the long lingering kiss of lovers. They went to dances at the Legion and enjoyed live theater when a show came to town.

Tom and Susan's children were growing fast and were both in school. Tommy was a wiz at mathematics and Grace just loved history. She wanted to know about every country in the world and vowed that when she was old enough she would visit every one of them. Tommy grew to be a big boy; the biggest in his class. One day he came home from school with a black eye. Susan said to him, "What on earth have you been up to?" He said, "Well gee mom, I got in a fight with one of the boys." "What were you fighting over?, she asked. "Well, this guy swiped a sandwich out of my lunch pail and I took a swipe at him. Don't worry mom, I bloodied his nose and he took off." Susan said, "Just wait till your father hears about this Tommy Epston!" When Tom came home from work he listened to his son's story and said, "I am going to pay a visit to your school and get to the bottom of this. I don't want to hear any more about you getting into fights at school. Are we understood Jimmy?" "Yes father, I understand but what am I to do if I am being pestered by some brat?" Tom replied, "I will take that up with your teacher. Now eat your supper and get to your homework." That was all that was said at that time.

Tom phoned the school and made an appointment to see the principal and Tommy's teachers. On the following Tuesday Tom and Susan went to the school. Apparently young Tommy had been involved in a couple of other squabbles with other boys and usually came out on top. He had also been using profane language in the hallways. The school councilor had spoken to Tommy. Could it be that he was a class bully? The principal said, "I will look into it and try to get to the bottom of it." Tommy was getting very good marks in his school work but did not seem to be a very happy boy in recent months. The previous year he had been an honor student. Now what could have made the change in him?

Tommy was now fifteen and had grown to be quite a big boy. He was good at sports and, in fact had been signed on to the football team. Something was bugging him and he didn't want to talk about it. Susan had a way with him and when they were alone she confided in him and said, "Tommy, you know that you can always talk to your mother. You know that your father and I want only the best for you. Now just tell me what is bothering you and maybe we can correct it before you get into any more trouble." Tommy squirmed in his chair and blurted out, "Some of the guys have been teasing me about Jane Simpson. She lives on the other side of town and they think she is a bad girl. I like her and we eat our lunch together. I think she is OK." Susan said, "Oh that is what it is about! Well now Tommy, have you tried ignoring the other boys? Jane is a very pretty girl and maybe they are jealous. I think you are strong enough willed to get over it and you certainly can continue to be friends with Jane. You can have her over if you like." Susan gave him a big hug and told him that if he had any troubles that she and his father would do what ever they could to help him.

That night when Susan and Tom were alone, Susan said, "You know Tom, I think our son has a crush on the Simpson girl. You know the one. She sings in the Church choir. I think he will be all right now I have spoken to him. You remember the crush you had on me." "Ah Yes." Said Tom "I think I would have blacked an eye or two if anybody tried to take you away from me." Jimmy Bette was in his last year of high school. He had become a first class goalie on the junior hockey team. He was not as fast a skater as the other players but was very quick in goal and had a few *shut-outs* to his credit. He now wanted to go on to University and take up pharmacy. He got a great deal of support from his grandfather who was a pharmacist. Sally was quite excited about her son going on with his education. It would mean that he would have to go to Vancouver or Victoria and the cost would be of some concern. Jimmy, *Bets* to his buddies, was an ambitious lad and determined to work his way through university. He stocked shelves in the local Safeway in his off hours from school and also took on odd jobs when he could get them. In the spring there was a big demand for garden tilling. Sally and Dave put up some money to buy a Roto-tiller, a new power machine that had recently come on the market.

The tilling jobs came on thick and fast. As soon as he started on one the neighbors would come over to watch and wanted their gardens done too. He didn't have to do any advertising and he had to set up a timetable to get all the jobs in correct order. Most of the time it meant going from one yard to the next, so he didn't need a truck to haul the machine around. In the first year he made enough money to pay off the machine and also save enough to pay his tuition and lodging for the first month or two. He came home one evening with a rag around his hand. Sally looked at it and asked, "What on earth have you done to your hand?" Jimmy replied, "It's nothing mom; just a few blisters from steering the tiller around." She doctored it up for him and insisted that he get a pair of work gloves and wear them.

In September Jimmy was off to the University of British Columbia in Vancouver. He found lodgings with an elderly couple, Mr. and Mrs. Smith. They were from England and had a very strong Yorkshire accent. It took Jimmy a long time to get used to it but he got along very well with them. He had a comfortable room overlooking the ocean and ate his meals with them. Mrs. Smith made a bag lunch for him to take to University. The campus was not far from there so he could walk to and from school. Jimmy was able to get some second-hand books from the campus book store so it looked like a very good start for the young freshman.

Sally and Dave continued with their art work, spending many hours together, seeking out scenes to paint. One night after a long stroll in the forest Dave suggested that they go out for supper. He selected the Prestige Restaurant, the nicest one in town. He had the foresight to reserve a table for the occasion. Sally changed into her favorite evening dress and they soon arrived at the Prestige in Dave's red sports car. After a delicious seafood dinner they sipped champagne by the flickering light of a single candle on their table. David said to her, "Sally, I have known you for some time now and when we are not together I just can't keep you out of my mind. I think I have been in love with you from the first night we met." In a formal manner he dropped to one knee and said, "Sally, I want you to be my wife.

Please, will you marry me?" At the same time he produced a beautiful diamond ring. Sally broke into tears of joy and said, "Of course I will marry you Dave. I have been waiting for this moment for a long time."

The next step was to inform Jimmy and Shelly. This was little surprise to Jimmy. When Sally phoned him his reply was simply, "Well it's about time mom." Shelly, now seventeen, didn't quite know what to say at first. She was used to seeing them together as friends but hadn't thought of them getting married. After a brief hesitation she said, "Mom, I think it is a wonderful idea. When is the wedding? I am too old to be your flower girl but maybe I could be a bridesmaid. Oh, I am so excited. Dave, Can I call you daddy? She gave them both a big hug and when the thrill of it all died down a bit, Shelly asked, "Where will we live?" Dave calmed her by saying, "Shelly, we have not even discussed that yet but I think we can include you in our decision." Shelly didn't know what to think of her mom remarrying and felt, perhaps a little insecure. She thought the world of Dave but would she be left out in the cold? She loved her mother dearly and couldn't even guess what it would be if she lost her. Losing her father had been a tragedy for her and this loomed up in her mind as an even worse disaster. Sally noticed the change in her daughter and felt perhaps a little guilt. She went to Shelly's room and sat on the bed beside her. She embraced Shelly and assured her that she and Jimmy would always be her first love and that she and Dave would always place the needs of her children at the very top. This quelled the tears that had come to Shelly's eyes and she smiled as she said, "Thank you mom, I feel much better now. Jimmy and I want you to be happy and as long as we can be a family forever my life will be filled to the brim." They sat for a long time in silence until Shelly started to nod off. It had been a long day for Sally as well as she sank into her own bed she fell into a deep and contented sleep.

Finally the wedding date was set for late April. Jimmy would be home from University, ending his first year. After the wedding he would go back to Victoria for the spring semester and get a couple more courses under his belt. He arrived back in Carebrook a few days before the wedding. Dave and he went fishing for a day, giving them a chance to get to know each other. They exchanged thoughts about the future and even talked about where the home would be. Would it be in town at his moms place or in the country at Dave's place? Jimmy thought it would be nice if they could keep the place in the country as a get-away and live in town, at least until Shelly was finished school. This made sense to Dave and he said, Sally and I will talk it over and try to do what is best. Jimmy had decided to take his tiller back to Vancouver and he could probably make enough money to work his way through another year. Dave said, "Jim, don't you worry about money for your university. If you need money I will see that it is there for you. All you have to do is ask." They didn't catch any fish that day but both agreed that it was a super fishing trip.

This wedding was to be far different from Sally's first

one. It would be well planned and for certain, the Church would be full. It was not to be a lavish wedding; just traditional with a reception and dance to follow. Sally opted to wear a pretty dress rather than a wedding gown. Dave wore a dark suit purchased for the occasion. They were a grand looking couple. As a surprise, Shelly sang Ava Maria during the signing of the register. As they emerged from the Church there was a goodly shower of rice rained down on them. They were congratulated by friends and relatives and then proceeded to the photography studio for pictures. The reception dinner and dance was held at the Prestige Hotel where the happy couple would occupy the bridal suite for their first night.

The following afternoon there was a gift opening at the club house by the lake. It was a chance for friends and relatives to chat and enjoy a time away from the loud music and scurry of the night before. Sally was radiant with her long blond hair and comely figure for her age.

Jimmy and Shelly were very proud of their mother and were at her beck and call for anything she wanted.

The next morning Jimmy drove the couple to Kelowna Airport where they would take a flight to Vancouver and then change planes to Los Angeles. This is where they would spend a two-week honeymoon. Of course Shelly came along to see them off. On the way home Jimmy and Shelly got to compare notes and both agreed that their mother was probably the happiest lady in the town of Carebrook. They talked about their own romantic adventures. Shelly said, "I have no steady boy friend right now and I am too busy with my dancing and drama to get involved. Oh yes; I have dates with a few of the boys but certainly nothing serious." Jimmy said, "You know what! I am going to call up Peggy as soon as we get home. Do you know if she is dating?" Shelly replied, "I haven't seen her lately but as far as I know she is still going to our school and she is still in the choir."

Jimmy ventured, "Shelly, are you sure you don't have some guy in your sights. You sure are a good looking sister to me." Shelly chuckled and replied, "Oh Jimmy you are such a flatterer. To answer your question, there are a couple of good looking guys in the drama class but I don't think they notice me that much." Jimmy suggested that she try a little flirting but Shelly said, "Don't be silly Jimmy; the time will come some day but not right now. I am in a big play right now and have to spend all the time I can on that."

As they arrived in town they could smell the lilacs that were now in full bloom. It seemed to be the vogue to have lilac hedges at this time. There also seemed to be an abundance of dandelions growing in peoples' lawns and in the boulevards. As they turned into the driveway they could see that it was obvious that Tom Epston had kept his promise and was still attending to Sally's yard. It was the showpiece of the block.

Joe and Beth and their family had been at the wedding and were thrilled to see Sally happily married again. They had always kept a lookout for her and were ready to help her if needed. Tom had a good job with forestry and still lived in the house at the end of the lane. It would never lose that name in Carebrook. Tom had sold a portion of the land and a new house had been built on it but Tom and Susan still had full access to the creek and the lake. This, they would never give up. Sally and Dave were frequent visitors and Sally always wanted to stroll along the creek-side and watch the minnows and other water creatures. This walk also had a sentimental meaning for Tom. Of course his dog Ruff was long gone but Tom had a new dog now. It was a golden retriever named Hunter. This dog seemed to love Sally just as much as Ruff had.

Chapter Eleven

Becky and John now had three children Fred, Jackie, and Carol. They were growing now, too fast it seemed. John adored his children, especially when they were learning to walk and talk. This family had moved into a comfortable three-bedroom home in a new development on the east side of town. John was now a foreman at the mill and Becky worked at a day-care facility. When the children were small she was able to take her own children there so all worked out fine. As they grew older she could leave them at home. They were well behaved and responsible enough to be on their own for a short period of time.

One evening Freddy went to his room early and as Becky went to the kitchen to put on the kettle for tea she heard a strange noise coming from Freddy's room. She knocked on his door and when she entered Freddy was sitting at his desk, apparently doing his homework. She asked him about the strange noise and in a very embarrassed voice he said, "It is nothing mom." In an instant she knew what it was and said, "Oh Freddy your voice is breaking. You are getting a man's voice. I suppose we should start calling you Fred." He replied, "I guess so. I was just practicing to see what it sounds like. I guess I will have to give up the Church choir." Becky said. "Of course you won't. You will just have to change positions."

After the children had all gone to bed John and Becky chuckled over having a teen-age son and talked about his future. Certainly he would have to go on to college after graduation from high school. John did not have a college education and wished only the best for his children. He had a wonderful savings plan at work just for that purpose. The company would match any amount that he had deducted for education.

Jackie and Carol were younger and in middle-school. They were just over a year apart in age and both were very bright in school. Carol always said, "I want to be a teacher when I grow up." Jackie was a bit of a tom-boy and wanted to work on a ranch. She was crazy about horses and often took a walk to the nearest farm to see the animals. Sometimes Becky was a bit nervous if Jackie was a bit late in returning home. However she was a strong girl and could probably look after herself Jackie sometimes got invited to come to the farm house by Mrs. Brown. She and her husband Bill had farmed here for the past twenty years and were a highly respected couple in the community. On one visit to the farm Jackie was introduced to a young lad who had been hired by the Browns to help with the chores. The boy's name was Gary White. He was a good looking young fellow with red hair and a face covered in freckles. Jackie liked him instantly. As they chatted Gary asked Jackie, "Do you know how to ride a horse?" She replied, "No, I have never had the chance but I would love to try." Gary said, "I will ask Mr. Brown if we can take a couple of his horses and I will help you to learn." With Mr. Brown's permission they went to the barn and took the two horses out to the coral. Gary showed her how to put the saddle and the bridle on. First he instructed her to lead the horse around the coral so they would become accustomed to one another. Jackie was a bit nervous when it came time for her to climb onto the saddle. Gary led the horse around the coral a few times before letting her go by herself. He was very patient as he gave instructions and as she alit he told her that the next lesson would be out in the pasture.

Jackie rushed home and was just bursting as she told her mother all about her adventure. She was convinced now that she wanted to live on a ranch. John listened in with interest and was quite pleased that his daughter had found such an interest. He thought to himself, "This is going to wind up costing me money." His guess proved to be quite accurate. One Sunday evening, after a day at the farm, Jackie asked her father if she could get a horse of her own. "Mr. Brown will let me keep it at the farm and he said that I could buy the yearling colt. It won't be very long before it is big enough for me to ride." John replied, "Not too fast young lady. I will go and see Mr. Brown and see what he has to say."

That night Becky and John talked it over and decided that it may be a very good thing for their daughter to have such an interest. Later that week John paid Bill Brown a visit. At first sight he saw that it was a very well kept farm and he liked Bill Brown. In the end they made a deal on the pony and Bill promised to oversee Jackie's training. The horse could be kept there for a very modest cost of boarding.

Carol was a typical teen-ager. Like all others she swooned over the likes of the Beatles and Elvis Presley. She was doing very well at school and still wanted to be a teacher. Carol was very popular with her peers and when she had some of her friends over the house was full of giggles and a tendency to accompany it with loud music. There was a rumpus room downstairs for them but there were times when Becky had to call down for less noise. John liked classical music and found it a bit difficult to understand the modern trends. During this time Sally had become involved with a boys and girls club. She was very well liked by the members. They called her Aunt Sal. She organized various programs for them, including nature hikes and the odd camp-out. Shelly often accompanied them as a chaperone and a leader. In the summer months they packed tents and made camp at one of the lakes in the area. Dave usually helped with transportation and setting up camp. He also gave safety lessons on camping in the wild. There were wild animals in the woods and special precautions had to be taken in storing food. Camp fires had to be strictly controlled and the camp sites had to be left tidy and clean. Sometimes they were able to take a couple of canoes with them and there was plenty to learn about using them safely. Dave stressed the fact that they should never be more than a stones throw from the shore. He gave instructions on how to sit in a canoe and what to do if it capsized. Lifebelts were an essential for anybody going out in a boat or a canoe. He gave lessons on fishing including preparing the fish for cooking. All members were responsible for gathering firewood and cleaning up the campsite.

In the meantime Sally taught them sanitation, cooking on a campfire, and safety when hiking in the woods. Very often the girls would seek out Aunt Sal for a bit of counseling with regard to personal matters. She seemed to have the answers to any problem. Sometimes one of the younger ones would get homesick and it was Sally who got them settled down. She also taught first aid and often was there to patch up a scratch or a bruise.

In the winter months the club outings were usually cross-country ski trips and were only day trips. The same rules applied as far as protecting the environment were concerned. One of the local farmers organized sleigh rides and the youngsters had a wonderful time on these excursions. A deal was made with the local bus company and those that could go took the trip to Golden Star Ski Resort for a day of down-hill skiing. Very often the club met at the club house by the lake and enjoyed an evening of singing or just hanging out and enjoying the big fireplace. They were a well respected group in the community and parents felt quite secure with Sally and Dave in charge.

Chapter Twelve

In his job with forestry Tom Epston was often called upon to travel to other parts of British Columbia. In the summer of 1960 he was sent up to an area north of Prince George to investigate an infestation of the pine beetle. This would mean extensive travel into uninhabited woodlands. With companion Jerry, they set out in a four-wheel-drive truck well equipped with survival gear and an ATV. It was not long before they learned what they had to contend with. There were large areas of muskeg and there were clouds of black flies. On the first day in the bush they set up a base camp that consisted of a large tent, sleeping cots, bed-rolls, a camp stove, and a good supply of food. Of course they were in bear country and had to be very particular about storing their food. When they traveled into the woods they carried their rifles and bear spray. Both were well trained in survival procedures and they were both in top physical condition.

Although the area had been surveyed from the air it was still necessary to make a closer investigation from the ground. Both men carried two-way radios so that they could keep in contact. By the end of the first week they had learned to cope with the black flies as best they could and they got into camp routine. They took turns at cooking and made up some mighty fine meals. There was a creek near their camp and they caught a few trout to add to the menu. One morning the men set out following the creek and marking trees that were infested. They came upon a path that was used by forest animals to come down to water. As they were walking up the path they heard a rustle in the woods and soon recognized it as a bear. She had a cub with her and when she saw Tom she reared up on her haunches and made threatening growls. Tom backed away slowly and that seemed to end the situation. Later in the day as they were returning to camp they found themselves situated between the bear and her cub. This was not a good place to be. This time the mother bear came charging at them. Tom used the bear spray which deterred her for the moment. They were able to back away and head down the trail. Just when they thought they were clear the bear charged after them and caught Jerry with a swipe across the calf of his leg. Just at this moment the cub cried out and the mother turned and ran to its rescue. Tom was able to get Jerry to his feet and they managed to get back to their camp. The lacerations in Gerry's leg were quite deep and he certainly needed medical attention. Tom bandaged him up and was able to slow the bleeding. He got on the radio and contacted search and rescue in Prince George. About an hour later they heard a helicopter overhead and Tom directed them to a small clearing beside the campsite. The medics fixed jerry's leg up and took him on board for the trip to the hospital. Tom contacted his regional office and was ordered to pack up camp and get back to Prince George. When he arrived in Prince George he found Jerry to be in good shape in the hospital and looking forward to getting back in the bush. This was not to be as both men were ordered back to home base and Tom was back with his family.

After this experience it didn't take much persuasion to get Tom to accept an office job at the central headquarters where he was in charge of research into forest infestations, a job he wanted in the first place. As he told his family, "I never want to be faced by an angry bear again." Susan was very thankful to have Tom back home in Carebrook.

Tom and Susan Epston were soon back into their usual routine, enjoying the summer months. They now had a small holiday trailer and continued to take weekend trips to nearby lakes. By this time most of the lakes had good campsites and the fishing was great. There was nothing like a good feed of rainbow trout cooked over a camp fire.

Tommy and Grace were now older and felt that they had better things to do with their weekends than go camping with mom and dad. They were involved with their friends and spending time in their own sporting events. Grace loved playing on the girls' softball team. They played other teams in town as well as those from neighboring communities. They were a good bunch, often camping out or going to the local dances. Of course she had her music to keep her busy. Tommy had his friends too. He played a bit of football and sometimes played hardball on a pick-up team. He and a couple of buddies spent a lot of time fishing and just having fun at the lake. Tommy wanted to have a motorcycle. He got a job at the local Shell service station pumping gas. It gave him some spending money but he saved most of it to buy that bike. One day he asked his dad if he could borrow fifty bucks to top off what he had saved. Dad gave him a good talk on money matters and the importance of staying out of debt. He loaned his son the money and the next day there was a brand new red motorbike in the driveway. Every day he had to wash it and shine it up and look after it just like his buddies looked after theirs.

They were a great bunch of boys and often spent hours in the Epston rumpus room playing their modern time favorites on the stereo. Elvis Presley was the favorite of the time. Sometimes Susan had to remind them about the volume.

In the meantime Jackie, Becky & John's daughter, was spending a lot of time at the Brown farm. She could now ride her pony and was taking riding lessons from Gary White. The two of them would race across the pasture and often disappeared in the wooded area beside the lake. Jackie was now seventeen and had grown to be a beautiful young lady. She was quite different from Carol in that she had lovely auburn hair; not the blond of her brother and sister.

Late one night Becky and John had just got home from a weekend of camping, Jackie came in apparently in great distress. She said, "There has been a terrible accident at the farm. Gary and I were riding in the pasture when Gary noticed a strange bull was in with Mr. Brown's cattle. It had broken through the fence from the neighbor's place. Gary tried to separate it from the herd and the bull suddenly charged and hit Gary's horse broadside. The horse stumbled and fell on Gary's leg and broke it. He is in the hospital .Please could you drive me there? I want to see him." Becky said, "Of course we will but just a short visit." In a flash she was in the car and they were on their way. By the time they got there Gary's leg was in a cast and he was resting in bed. On the way home from the hospital John said to Jackie, "This boy seems to mean a great deal to you." She replied, "We are very good friends and he has taught me a whole lot about horses. He is a swell guy."

On Saturday Jackie went to see Gary in the hospital and as she sat by his bed he asked her if she could reach him a glass of water. She had to reach across the bed to the table. As she leaned over him her auburn hair fell across his face and as she pulled herself up his eyes fell upon her abundant cleavage. A huge feeling of excitement welled up in him. He took her hand and said, "Jackie, I want you to be my girlfriend forever." They held hands tightly and Jackie said, "Of course, I already am and I can hardly wait until you are all healed up and we can go riding together." So it was that this shy farm boy finally was able to say what had been stored in his heart for a long time.

When Jackie went to the farm she said to Mr. Brown, "I will come over and do Gary's chores every day until he is able to carry on." Bill Brown thanked her very much and agreed to pay her for it. He also sensed that there may be more than a friendship between these two.

By now Fred was a star on the football team. Much of his time was spent in the gymnasium. He had grown to be a big boy and luckily managed to come through the football season with only minor injuries. He didn't miss a game. His hope was to be noticed by a coach from the senior league. Like most boys he dreamed of playing in the NFL. He was popular with the girls but didn't have a steady girlfriend.

Grace Epston carried on with her music. She frequently got requests to play the harp or sing at special occasions. So far there had been no evidence of romance in her life. She loved what she was doing and was getting well paid by those who requested her to perform. She continued taking music lessons and was forever coming home with new pieces to practice. Her voice training in the choir brought out the best in her lovely singing voice. As she prepared for the fall festival she spent more and more time at the piano and of course her harp. It was a joy to have such talent in the home.

One night Grace came home from choir practice and seemed to be acting rather strange. Susan asked her, "What have you been up to Grace? You look like the cat that swallowed the canary." Grace couldn't seem to sit still. She said, "Oh mom you will never guess what happened tonight. Jeff Thompson asked me if I would go to the music festival with him. He is going to pick me up in his new car on Saturday night.' Of course Susan knew his mom and dad and she said, "That is wonderful Grace. Perhaps you should invite him over so we can meet him." Two nights before the festival, a very shy young man rang the doorbell. John answered the door and invited Jeff to come in. As soon as he saw Grace, it was obvious that this was more than a casual friendship. Jeff was a clean-cut lad. He didn't smoke and was very courteous when speaking to Grace's mom and dad. While he was there Jeff played the piano and Grace sang and played the harp. It was an enjoyable evening for all of them. Later Tom said to Susan, "It looks as though our young lady has finally noticed a boy." Susan replied, "I think he is a very nice boy and I hope they will continue to date.

About a month after this Grace saw her brother Tom sitting with a girl at a basketball game. He had his arm around her and seemed to be paying more attention to her than the game. When they got home Grace started teasing Tom, as sisters will do. "Who's the young chick you had at the game Tom?" He replied, "None of your business! Are you a spy or something?" "Oh, come on Tom what's her name," teased Grace. Tom said, "Well, if you must know, her name is Peggy Long. She was in my class at school and she is also going to Okanagan College with me. Is there anything else you want to know?"

It was not long before Peggy was a guest in the Epston home. Peggy was a lovely girl and she was studying to be a teacher.

There was a shortage of teachers at this time as the "baby boomers were starting their families and all communities seemed to be growing by leaps and bounds. New schools were being built and whole new housing developments were springing up. At this time a new house could be purchased for around $50,000.00. There was a demand for tradesmen in all sectors of industry. In a very good move the federal government funded industrial training courses in many of the high schools. It was called vocational training. Fully equipped shops were set up for automotives, carpentry, plumbing, welding, general metals, and electrical. Also included was cooking, sewing, drafting. and even television arts. The program was a huge success. Students who were not academically inclined often excelled in the vocational program. Where did the teachers come from? A program was set up whereby journeyman tradesmen could be funded by the government to get their first two years of university toward a degree in education and get a temporary teaching certificate to start teaching in the schools. Most of them continued their university courses in night school and summer school to complete their education degree. Typically these teachers started their teaching careers in their thirties and forties. Under this program a student could graduate from high school and challenge the first year apprenticeship exam on their way to a journeyman's certificate. Thousands of them did this and filled the shortage of tradesmen in these industries.

When this program first started there was a little difficulty in integrating the the vocational students with the academic students. Some of the academic kids looked down on the trades kids. There were only a few confrontations but the feeling did exist. The academic teachers tended to sit separate from the vocational teachers in the teachers' cafeteria and staff rooms. However this did not last very long. They soon found out that very useful items could be produced in the shops. For example the welding shop could build utility trailers or make repairs to many metal objects. The carpentry shop was soon making things for academic teachers. They only had to pay for materials and so it was in all the other the other shops. The work was done as a learning project by the students under close supervision of their teachers. It was not long before there was harmony between staff members as well as the students.

In these days there was great rivalry in sports between schools. The physical education departments looked after all sports including baseball, football, hockey, basketball, swimming, weight lifting, and many other non-academic courses. All of these activities earned credits toward their high school diplomas.

Starting in the sixties the students were becoming very self conscious about their dress and were ever ready to take up any fad that came along. One of the fashions was to wear tight blue jeans about the bum and ragged legs splotched with bleach stains. Girls dressed alike. Very few of the girls came to school in dresses or skirts. The boys grew their hair half way down their backs. Some had expensive styling and others didn't bother to comb their hair at all. Most of them wore ball caps placed on their heads backwards and wore them in class.

Teachers also became very lax about their dress. Traditionally a male teacher wore a suit and tie to school. The ladies wore dresses or suits. During this era the ladies changed over to wearing slacks and blouses. The men also became very casual in their dress. A few of the male teachers even grew long hair and wore blue jeans in an attempt to emulate the students. With that discipline took a severe downward turn. Students still graduated and as they went into the work world they soon found that they had to moderate their ways in order to get good positions on the job.

These fads quickly spread from the large centers to the smaller communities because of television advertising, bill boards, and other forms of visual advertising. The clothing industry kept tab on the latest fads and were able and willing to take advantage of it. Entertainers took a leading role in the promotion of these fads. Carebrook was no exception to the acceptance of these fads and the behavior that went along with it.

. This was the time when drugs started to become popular with the school students. Marijuana was the drug of the day. Although it was an illegal substance it spread very quickly. The drug dealers knew how to get to the kids and the results were tragic. One can imagine what it is like to try and teach a bunch of glassy eyed kids. A great deal of controversy arose as to whether marijuana should be legalized or not and still continues to the time of this writing. It has been proven that drugs have been the cause of a huge surge in crime including theft and even murder and suicide. Politicians and the public at large seem to be at a loss for a solution. The contention of the writer is that soft drugs only lead to harder drugs and legalizing it will do nothing to solve the problem In 1957 Sputnik was launched by the Russians which led to the space race between Russia and the United States. The United States put the first man in space. At this time the space craft came back to earth being slowed by parachute and it splashed down in the Atlantic Ocean off the Florida Coast. A floatation device kept the capsule afloat until the occupants were recovered. The Russian's space craft made a hard landing and it was suspected to be very hard on the astronaught. It was not long before the United States landed a man on the moon.

The space age brought about many changes in the way families lived. The super electronics required for space travel trickled down into common household goods. Major appliances started having computer boards and such things as washing machines could be programmed to the type of fabric being washed.

Times were ever changing: the way people expressed themselves, newspaper reporting, many new words pertaining to the computer age, and even the way people viewed life in general. This may well be called the "got to have age." The credit card era was well established. A person could buy anything. Just pull out the credit card and worry about paying at a later date. For some people it was a very precarious way of handling their finances. In a very short time one could be hopelessly in debt. With the high interest charges a person could pay for an item many times over before actually owning it. The wise spender would pay the credit bill in full before the due date and not have to pay any interest. In this way the credit card was a card of convenience. For instance when traveling a person could put all his travel expenses on the card and pay it up in one lump sum on return home. In an emergency the credit card could at least buy some time to get things sorted out. It had other advantages as well. A person didn't have to carry large amounts of cash. One could take advantage of good sale prices. It was also a great boon to merchants and service people. They didn't have to give credit nor did they have the huge expense of trying to collect unpaid bills. The majority of people used their credit card at the gas pump. Added to this came the debit card whereby a person could access his/her bank account and pay for goods directly without having to handle cash. It also saved the hassle of having to get a check approved at every transaction. The older folks, i.e. Sally or Tom knew about harder times and tried to impress upon their children the value of caution when using a credit card.

It would be amusing to watch a young person shopping for groceries and then watch an older person who had come through hard times. The young person would go up and down the aisles loading items into the basket without even looking at the prices. An older person would be much slower and more deliberate at comparing prices and looking for the items that were on sale. Perhaps the younger generation had a freer style of life.

The children of the WW2 veterans were known as the baby boomers. It was a time when service people were returning home, getting married, and having children. It was as though they were making up for lost time. Very little was regarded concerning birth control. A family of six or more children was common. As these children grew up many new schools had to be built as well as other family resources.

Parents wanted their children to have everything, thinking back in the times they were growing up. For instance pre-war children may be considered lucky to get one gift at Christmas time.

Now, in post-war times, the stores were filled with a wide variety of toys for children. As time went on toys that could be remotely controlled became the norm. All sorts of electronic games were filling the store shelves. No longer was an ordinary doll acceptable. It had to be able to talk and do other things like walk and cry and suck on a soother. Students were turning to the use of calculators rather than the old method of learning mathematics. Schools were filling with computers. The home computer was becoming commonplace. The older folks deemed it too difficult to try to learn to use a computer and just gave up. They were amazed to see a five-year-old turning on the computer and use it like an expert, even teaching grandpa how to use it.

The computer, not only was found in the average home.

Bill Brown had a computerized milking station on his farm. The feeding program for farm animals was all figured out by computer. The horse had long been replaced by the tractor but now technology came in to play. Tractors now had air conditioned cabs equipped with radios. The farmer could now adjust the machines he was using with a flick of a switch. He now was rid of the hard labor of the old days. Machines were equipped with hydraulic systems that took all the hard work of lifting heavy weights. Instead of laboring every day of the year to keep his farm up he could take a month off in the winter and take a holiday in a warm climate. They joined the flock of *snowbirds* heading for places like Arizona and Hawaii. Many of the farmers built large modern homes comparable with city homes. Technology allowed larger farms and many times more efficient farming methods that yielded higher profits so that they could enjoy this style of life.

Jackie and Gary were now planning to get married in the spring. Bill Brown had taught Gary all about running the farm and he told the young couple that after they were married they could have a mobile home set up in his yard. They could buy their home for a fraction of the price of a house and it would have all the modern conveniences, including a home computer. This was a wonderful wedding present for them. Between the two of them they could look after the farm while the Browns were on vacation.

A new generation was well on its way. Sally and Dave were grandparents and so were Joe and Beth Epston. By the way things were going it wouldn't be too long before they would be great-grandparents. They were ever interested in what all of them were doing and took great pride in the young ones. All of their children had good jobs and were raising their families as they themselves had been brought up. They often said that the grandchildren had too much and that they were spoiled. The main thing was that they were loved by their parents and disciplined to make good citizens. They had all done well in school and most of them had gone on to higher education. Strangely enough none of the grandchildren smoked. For sure they had all tried it, and maybe some marijuana as well but all had decided that it was not the way to go. All the cousins socialized together and then there were the great get-togethers at the club house by the lake. They skied together and went on camping trips together as well. Seldom one would find such harmony in a family.

Students were turning to the use of calculators rather than the old method of learning mathematics. There was a house a block from Joe Epston's place that came under suspicion by the neighbors. A group of young people lived there. Cars were coming and going all hours of the day and night. The blinds were always down and the occupants were seldom seen. The lawn was not cut for weeks and it became an eyesore in the neighborhood. One day Joe just got fed up with it and went to the RCMP Office. He told them of his suspicions and they informed him that the house was already under surveillance and would likely be raided in a day or two. They wanted to catch the ring leaders. Sure enough, when they raided the house, they found it to be a grow operation. Fifty marijuana plants were seized along with all the equipment. The electrical meter had been by-passed and the house was an absolute wreck. The culprits were taken away to cells at the police station and then to a provincial jail to await trial. This was only the beginning of a large number of grow-ops being discovered in the interior of the province.

Along with marijuana came harder drugs and it wasn't long before drug addicts were hanging around down town and in the parks. They had to have their drugs and with no source of income they resorted to breaking into homes and businesses and stealing money and valuables that could be sold so they could buy their drugs. There was a faction of the public that tried to promote the legalization of marijuana so that it could be purchased in stores and it could be grown in any garden legally. This remains a bone of contention.

Chapter Thirteen

Carebrook continued to grow and prosper. A new recreation facility was built down town, complete with a full-size swimming pool. A new modern bowling alley was built, along with a billiard parlor. The main street was repaved and a new hotel with 60 rooms sprang up. It even had a meeting hall large enough to accommodate small conventions. Real estate prices soared. Now an average three bedroom house cost over one hundred thousand dollars. A large area near the lake was developed into acreages and these were quickly snapped up by those who wanted a more rural place to live. A family could now own a horse and it wasn't long before a riding club was established. Riding also became a fad, especially for young girls. They looked mighty smart in their riding habit.

By this time Jim and Peggy were dating regularly and were often seen at the bowling alley or enjoying a swim in the pool. Jim had purchased a second-hand dodge pick up. It was his pride and joy. He was forever polishing it and buying new accessories for it. It had a radio in it but of course he needed to have a more sophisticated set with six speakers and he could be heard coming a block away. This was the modern way. He was a good driver and did not drink so that Peggy's mom and dad felt that she was in good hands when she was with Jim.

It was not long before Jim proposed to her and presented her with a ring. They were out on the lake in a canoe. The sun was setting behind the Monashee mountains. A loon called out in the twilight and Jim stopped paddling in the middle of the lake. He said, "Peggy, I have something for you." as he handed the little jewel box over to her. She opened it and screamed out, "Jim, are you proposing to me?" He replied, "Yes Peggy, I want you to be my wife." As she answered him she almost upset the canoe. "Oh yes Jim, of course I will. I have been hoping for this day for a long time." They quickly paddled to shore and rushed home to the Thompson's home. Peggy tore into the house and displayed her ring to her mom and dad. This called for a celebration and they made a dinner date for the following evening. Of course Jim's mom and dad would have to be there too. Indeed it was a happy time when they all got together at the restaurant in the new hotel. Peggy announced that the wedding date would be two months from tonight. She had planned it all in her mind just waiting for this night. This would be a big wedding for this popular couple. Grace and Jeff were still dating but there was no sign that they were going to even think of wedding bells. They were busy with their music and Grace was preparing for a festival in Vancouver. Jeff was getting a little less enthusiastic about the music because it was taking too much of Grace's time and he was feeling a bit neglected. A week later Grace was off to Vancouver and Jeff went along too. The festival was a huge success for Grace. She got first place for her singing in two categories and second in the third. When she got back to her hotel she was exhausted but took time to phone home with the results.

Jeff sang in a duet with Grace and this is where they came in second. Jeff had an enjoining room but he stayed with Grace to enjoy a bottle of champagne to celebrate the occasion. Perhaps he stayed a little too long because hours later he awoke on Grace's bed with her in his arms. As they drove back to Carebrook the next morning Jeff again pleaded with Grace to ease up on the music for awhile. She seemed to look at it in a different light this time and she promised that she would She had accomplished what she wanted and would be content to meet her weekly commitments in Carebrook.

The wedding arrangements were going ahead for Tom and Peggy. The guest list counted 150 and it was to be a grand affair. Both of them had many friends and it was for certain the Church would be full. All went according to plan; the men in tuxedos and the ladies in their beautiful dresses. Peggy looked stunning in her white wedding dress. Tom surprised her when he showed her two plane tickets to Hawaii for a honeymoon. He had told her that they would be going to go to Vancouver for a week.

As time passed Jeff and Grace continued in their music but also were often seen strolling along the lake shore, hand in hand. The relationship seemed far more intimate than it had been in the past. There also seemed to be a change in Grace's relationship with her mother and dad. She was sleeping in most mornings and spent a lot of time in her room. Susan suspected that there was something not just right. She rapped lightly on Grace's door and when she opened it she found Grace sobbing on her bed. Susan asked, "What on earth is the matter Grace? You know you can always confide in me. Now, tell me please." Grace's sobbing grew into outright crying. She said, "Its Jeff and me. We love each other so much but have a problem. Yes mom, I am pregnant. It was that night in Vancouver. Are you going to tell dad?" "You know he will have to know. Now we will face this together," Susan consoled, holding her daughter close to her. They sat for some time in silence and at last Susan said, "That was three months ago. Have you seen the doctor?" "Yes I have and he says everything looks fine. Jeff and I want to get married but don't think we can afford it right now." "Don't worry Grace. Your father and I will see you through this. I expect you will keep the baby." "Oh yes, we just couldn't think of giving it up." By now Grace had stopped crying and the two women decided to wait till tomorrow to talk about plans for a wedding. Of course there was much more to be considered before such a step could be taken. What would Tom's reaction be? Would Jeff be ready to take such a step, and Jeff's parents too would have to come into the picture.

Prior to this time an unwanted pregnancy was kept secret and often the mother-to-be went away to stay with an aunt or a trusted friend until the baby was born. Many of these babies were adopted out and the people at home were none the wiser that anything had happened. By now it was more acceptable and so came the expression, "the unwed mother." These women could get some social benefits and so more of them kept their babies and they became "working mothers."

In some cases, when a girl got pregnant, she sought out somebody who would perform an abortion. If done properly all was well and the girl carried on as usual. Some of them suffered psychological problems over the fact that they had lost their baby. In a few cases a girl may try to abort herself and suffered disastrous physical damage. At this time there was a women's movement to try and legalize abortion. It wound up as a political agenda and doubt that it will ever be solved.

Jeff was relieved that Grace had told her parents and now it was up to him to see how much sympathy he would get at home. Of course they were shocked to hear that their quiet, shy son could get into this predicament, however they elected to support him and were glad to know that he was not abandoning the young lady. The two families got together to plan the wedding. After the wedding the young couple could stay with Tom and Susan until they found a place of their own and Jeff found a steady job. Grace made a bit of money from her performances but they would need more than that with a new baby.

Tommy was now bringing Peggy home for Sunday dinners and they spent many hours with their loud music in the downstairs family room. Susan had to remind him a few times to turn the volume down and he was quite good about it. It was not long after Grace had set her wedding date for June that Peggy was sporting a beautiful engagement ring. She and Tommy were both attending University in the fall for their last year so decided to wait until after their graduation day was over. How things were changing in the Epston household. Tom jr. would have a good job when he graduated and he had put some money aside from his garden tilling in the meantime. Like his father, he was a very responsible young man. Peggy was a blast. She was full of fun and everybody was laughing when she was around. She looked forward to the day when she could be a full time registered nurse. Grace and Jeff were married on a beautiful sunny day in June. They opted to go camping for their honeymoon. They borrowed Tom's tent and away they went in Jeff's car. On their return they told everybody what a wonderful time they had. A good start for them!

Chapter Fourteen

The town of Carebrook continued to grow rapidly. This put a large strain on the town finances because, as each subdivision was opened, the utilities had to expand with it. This caused concern among the citizens because it was necessary to raise property taxes. Once they saw the new amenities coming in they accepted it and only a few caused any amount of a stir. A second newspaper came in as well as a new television station.[CBC] A bid for a new arena was tabled for the time but would certainly come later as would a modern performing arts building.

There were other concerns as well. One of these was that the bulge in population would eventually put a huge strain on the health care system. Would there be enough money for old-age pensions or Canada pension plan payment? How could there ever be enough jobs to support such a bulge in the work force? They seemed to loose sight of the fact that these young people also added to the consumer pool. At the same time immigration was bringing thousands of people from Europe and other parts of the world. They had to be crowded into the work force as well. People complained that these immigrants were working cheap and taking all the jobs. What it resulted in was expansion of many large and small companies alike.

Those who really wanted to work could usually find work even if it was not their life's desire. Many started self – employment businesses and many of them expanded and increased job opportunities for others. These small businesses have been called the backbone of industry in Canada. A good example was Tommy Epston's garden tilling business. Had he wanted to pursue this business it could have grown into a large gardening and landscaping business requiring many new employees. However he chose to go the education route and went on to university, which assured him of a good income without the risks of a business. At this time it was said that one out of five small businesses failed. In earlier times it was very difficult to get loans from banks. As time went on many finance companies opened up but their interest rates ate up much of the profit made from the use of this money. Unless one had a good bit of money to invest to get the business going the chances of making a go of it were slim.

As time went on mortgages became easier to obtain and the financing of a home could be spread over twenty to thirty years. The problem was getting enough money for the down payment. Some borrowed money from a relative or friend but were now stuck with two mortgages rather than one. If he wanted to buy a car or new furniture he had to live very close to the line.

With the addition of children it could become very difficult to meet all the payments. So came the time that both husband and wife had to work in order to meet their commitments. This ushered in the beginning of day-care centers. Some couples split their working time so that one worked days and the other worked nights while the one that was at home looked after the children. Many families did this and seemed able to struggle on and raise their children and eventually work themselves out of the financial bind. There were also some that had to give up their homes and even have some of their assets seized because they just couldn't make a go of it. In spite of this the economy looked reasonably good and most of the people thrived. As for Carebrook, new industries came in and most of the people were employed and there were very few signs of poverty.

Joe Epston was getting up in years and preparing to retire. He had no financial worries because he had a good company pension to look forward to. His house was paid for and his children were doing well. Joe and Beth bought a motor home and planned to put it to good use as soon as he retired. Sally and Dave continued with their busy lives although Sally was starting to see a need to slow down a bit. She was still skiing but taking on the more gentle slopes. They still enjoyed taking the boat out on the lake and catching a few rainbow trout. On Sally's 65th birthday there was a great celebration. All the families got together at the club house and the party went on into the wee hours. By now Sally had to add a little hair color to hide a few gray ones starting to show. She was still a very attractive lady and was a leader in the community. She suggested to Dave that she should try out for city council but Dave talked her out of that one. He wanted her to continue with her art work and besides that he didn't want to share her attention with the public.

Jim Bette returned to University in September but he found Pharmacy very difficult. He was talking to Peggy over a cup of coffee one evening after the first month of study. He said to her, "Peggy, I just seem to be banging my head against a brick wall. I am not sleeping properly and I have been thinking about making a change." She asked, "What are you thinking of doing Jim?" "Well you know

Peggy; I did very well in my welding classes in high school and the more I think about it, the more I think that welding should be my career. It is a shorter course and I would be making good money during my apprenticeship. In two years I could be a full fledged journeyman welder." "And where would you go for that?" she asked. Well the first thing I would have to do is get a job as an apprentice. I would have to work on the job and go to a vocational institute for two months of each of the two years." Peggy didn't look very happy about it and asked, "What about us Jim?" Jim took her hand and said, "You know Peggy that I want us to get married as soon as possible and if I make this change we could probably be able to afford it in a few months time. Wouldn't a spring wedding be great?" "Oh Jimmy: I hope you are not giving up Pharmacy for that reason alone." He squeezed her hand and replied, "Of course not Peggy. I have been thinking of this change for some time now, even during the summer break. I want you to carry on with your career and we will make out fine. I may even be able to get a job right here and we don't even have to be apart except when I am at school. I don't want to do anything unless we both agree." Peggy took a deep breath and answered, "Jim, I will go along with what you think is best. You know that I want us to be married as soon as we can." This ended the conversation and they returned to their respective dormitories.

The next morning Jim made an appointment to see the Dean. He got in right away and told the Dean of his plans. Dean Jones was not pleased to lose Jim in the faculty but wished him well and stated that he would be welcome back any time. This was a time when educational opportunities were open to all ages. Jim made up his resume' which included his experience in high school. He had a strange feeling as he approached the employment bureau. He hesitated for a moment and then went in. He was interviewed by one of the counselors and was told that there was a fairly high demand for welders in the northern part of the Province where the oil industry was booming. She gave him the names of three firms that had recently been seeking workers.

Jim's next step was to seek out the offices of these companies and make appointments. The first one he went to wanted men in the north and they would call him when they were making selections. Jim went to the second place and it turned out to be a small local shop. The owner was very impressed with Jim's resume' and asked him how soon he could start work.

Jim replied very enthusiastically, "Could I come in tomorrow? I have been going to University and will have to get some suitable work clothes. That evening Jim took Peggy out for dinner and he was just bubbling to tell her that he would be working in a local shop and they could still see each other whenever their work gave them the time. So it was that Jim changed his vocation and he seemed much happier now. He had to really scrub his hands before a date because welding is not the cleanest job in the world. They often joked about it. Jim's first school session would start in February. Peggy yelled out, "Maybe we can get married when I am on spring break!" Jim said, "It sounds great to me. I am making pretty good money on the job and it will only get better as I progress with my apprenticeship. I will let you set the date Peggy." Their goodnight was a lingering one that night. Jim went to spend the last few nights night in the dorm and had to find a place to live by the weekend. He was very lucky to find a bachelor suite ten blocks from the university so everything was turning out wonderfully for both of them.

Whenever Jim and Peggy got the time they came home to Carebrook and stayed with Sally and Dave. There was usually a large gathering on these occasions. Sally was so interested in Jim's progress and kept asking the same question, "When are you two going to set the date for your wedding?" She was already making plans. They hoped to tie the knot at the end of the spring semester. Peggy would still have another year to go before graduation and she was determined to finish. Jim was going into his third year of his apprenticeship and doing very well. He loved his work and never regretted changing from Pharmacy. His work was so good that his boss gave him all the specialty jobs to do. His ambition to have his own rig but would have to wait until after he graduated as a journeyman welder.

Sally was starting to show her age now. Peggy remarked, "I see a couple of grey hairs mom." They had a good laugh over it and Sally reminded her, 'I'm nearly fifty you know, so I guess I will have to start using the dye bottle soon."

Sally and Dave were planning a tour of Europe and were getting passports and medicals and new luggage for the trip. Up to this time suitcases were hard covered but the new ones were made of a durable fabric. They were lighter and could hold more than the older ones. The common way to travel overseas was now by air. The passenger liners were being phased out except for special cruises. The cruise business was new and growing rapidly. These were luxury ships and passengers were pampered with every comfort possible. The food was exotic and entertainment on board was top quality. This would be the first long trip for both of them and their excitement grew as the day of departure drew near.

On the morning of departure Dave and Sally drove to Vancouver and left their car in "park and fly". They registered in at the airport and were soon soaring above the clouds. It was a long ride to Heathrow Airport in London and they were glad to get into a taxi to their hotel. The next morning they met their tour guide and were off by bus. This was a 14 day tour with a very busy agenda. They traveled to Belgium, Holland, and then down the Rhine to Switzerland. They were astounded at the beauty of the Alps, Lake Lucerne, and the rolling countryside on the road to Vienna. They took a ride in a gondola in Venice and toured the many famous places, i.e. churches, art museums, and other famous buildings. Sally and Dave had their sketch boards with them and knew they would have a lot of work to do when they got home. The tour took them down to Rome where they spent a few days and they marveled at the old ruins of structures that had been built centuries ago. Then it was north through olive groves and many old towns. In Pisa they climbed up the tower marveling that it still stands. They passed through the grape vine country of southern France to the gay city of Paris. They were in their glory as the visited the West Bank where artists display their works. They met some of the artists and even bought a couple of paintings. The Louvre was of special interest to them. Never before had they seen so many statues and grand old buildings. They took in a performance at the famous Opera and strolled down the Champs Elise'. It was a sad day when they had to leave this magnificent city. As the bus traveled westward they could see the monument at Vimy Ridge of WW1 fame where the Canadians turned the tide of the war resulting in the defeat of Germany. The bus took them aboard the ferry to England and they were soon back in London. After a couple of days of sight-seeing there they were back to the airport for the flight home. They had bags of pictures to show everybody and vowed that this would not be their last holiday to far-away lands.

Chapter Sixteen

As the twentieth century entered its last half the communication revolution sprang forth. From the time of the first radio signals to span the Atlantic Ocean at Signal Hill - [Marconi] communication has become almost instant. Fuelled by the need for faster communication during wartime our scientists made great strides, first by telephone, then cable, and then by radio. During wartime messages were sent from ship to ship by flashing lights in code. War dogs and pigeons were used to carry messages between headquarters and the troops in the trenches. Telephone lines were strung through very hazardous areas and were difficult to maintain. When wireless radio came into use communication became instant and spared the lives of many of these brave men. During WW2 when Tom was on his dangerous missions he relied on his radio set to guide him and to warn him of approaching danger. Most communications were transmitted by radio although dispatch riders and runners were still used. In modern times all printed matter can be sent and received by computer. Photography also played an important role. Pictures could be photographed from the air and transformed into actual maps. Targets for bombing raids were so accurately shown that a specific building could be picked out. At sea enemy submarines could be accurately detected by sonar.

In civil aviation there were huge strides in ground to air communication. In early times traffic was controlled by beams of colored lights from a control tower, a green light indicated permission to proceed on the ground or permission to land if in the air. A red light was a wave off or a stop signal, a flashing white or amber light meant to return to base. Traffic in seaports was controlled in a similar manner. After WW2 teletype allowed communication to be sent and received in actual print. This was closely followed by the computer. This technology advanced so quickly that by the time a computer reached the market, it was almost obsolete. E-mail became a common means of communication. The computer can also relay messages by voice.

Since the turn of the century the cell phone has become a common household tool of communication. It is portable and can be used almost everywhere. Most school children have a cell phone and can contact home or any of their friends in an instant. Communication between earth and outer space is commonplace. Television can be transmitted anywhere in the world by the use of satellites sent into orbit from earth. It is within the realm of possibility that it won't be long before automobile traffic will be controlled remotely, almost doing away with collisions and the death toll on our highways.

How did all this impact the people we are following? Many new words and expressions were entering our vocabulary. Music could be fed directly into the ears of our young people despite the warnings of later hearing loss. Seeing a person using a cell phone while walking down the street or driving a car became common place.... Instant communication. Did all this make life easier? Did it improve the quality of life? Some would say that it just made life faster: perhaps too fast. It may have made daily tasks easier but it also made way for much more activity to be crowded into a person's life. More people were showing up at the psychiatrist's office. Doctors now were prescribing medicines to keep their patients from nervous break downs. The pressures of every day life continued to grow.

Jim and Peggy were now married and saving money for a home. Peggy graduated as a registered nurse and Jim was now a journeyman welder. They were soon able to buy a house in Carebrook, not far from Sally's place. Peggy planned to work until they could save enough to start a family. Jim was looking around for a welding rig, a truck equipped with all his welding equipment so that he could travel to his work. He wanted to have his own business and take advantage of opportunities in the oil patch. It would mean being away quite a bit of the time but, if successful, he could set up his shop in Carebrook and hire welders to look after the field work. Sally and Dave were ever supportive of his ventures.

Jackie and Gary now had two children and remained on Bill Brown's farm. Bill was getting older and wanting to retire. He no longer did very much of the work on the farm. Gary was in charge and pretty much looked after the operation. Bill had purchased the neighboring farm and hired two more hands so everything there was working out well. Jackie took the two children down to the coral to get them used to the horses. Gary came in from the field one day and was astonished to see young Bobby in the saddle and Jackie leading the horse around the coral. He called out, "Jackie, what on earth are you doing?" Jackie just laughed and said, "He will be all right. I will see he doesn't fall." She had him fastened into the saddle. It wasn't long after that Bobby was riding on his own, but only in the coral. His little sister Jill was only one so she would have to wait another year before her turn came. Farm accidents were not uncommon when working with animals and machinery. Although Bill Brown had changed over from horses to tractors he still had a few horses and a small herd of cattle. By now the Department of Agriculture was offering safety courses for farmers and Bill always made sure that those working on his farm attended them. Bill often talked about retiring to a home in town but as he thought about it he didn't think he could cope with city life. He and his wife loved the country life and, after all, they had all the conveniences of a city home. Gary and Jackie were entrenched there now and even asked Bill if they could buy a couple of acres of his land and build a modern home on it. It would require the red tape of sub-dividing and Bill said he would consider it. Bill contacted the Land Titles Office the next time he was in town and was told that it would have to be a ten acre plot and would have to include a safe water supply. The latter would be no problem because there were two good wells on the farm, one that would be within the ten acre boundary. Bill called a meeting with the couple and made the proposal. With a wink of his eye he said, "You two have become part of my family and I will make you a deal. You pay for the paper work and it is yours." Of course Gary and Jackie were ecstatic. Jackie cried for joy and said, "Oh Mr. Brown I can't tell you how happy I am. I always wanted the country life and you are making it come true." On that same night Jackie announced that she was expecting another child and that maybe they could have the house built by the time the baby arrived. Bill brought out a bottle of wine to celebrate the event and it was near midnight before Jackie and Gary left for their trailer. They all were beaming from ear to ear as they said their good nights.

It didn't take long before the whole family knew about Jackie's great windfall. A party was arranged at the club house and everybody showed up for the celebration. Sally was on hand to make all the arrangements for food and to see that everything went perfectly. This party went on into the wee hours of the morning and everybody wished the couple every success and offered to help out in any way they could.

Joe and Beth Epston were there and Sally thought that Joe was looking a bit frail. He was retired of course but seemed to lack his usual high spirits. Sally took Beth apart and asked, "Is Joe all right? He looks very tired." Beth answered, "I didn't want to say anything but Joe went in for tests last week and they have found some cancer in him but he thinks it can be controlled for awhile anyhow. We can only hope." This was a shock but considering all the families in the group, they had been very lucky so far. As usual Sally offered to help out in any way she could.

Tom and Susan Epston were there, a little older but in their usual good spirits. Tom's sideburns were showing some gray but he was his usual happy self. Tom was now in full charge of his department and was often away lecturing at seminars and giving courses for new officers of the department. Susan was busy with grandchildren, ever fussing over them and perhaps spoiling them a bit. They just loved going over to grandma's place and scrounging a few cookies. No harm done, they were adorable kids. Tommy and Grace were frequent visitors there as well.

Sally and Dave still had the property by the lake but they were spending less time there now. As time changed they found a new interest. Dave came home one day with a hand full of brochures. They were brightly colored and showing views of tropical islands and grand resorts. Dave said, "Look at these. They are just waiting for you and me. Let's take a holiday to

a nice warm place this winter. We should be able to afford it."
Sally said, "what about our nice times at the cottage. Can we
afford both?" Dave replied, "I have been thinking about that
place and find it a bit hard to keep up along with this house,
I know we can sell it quite quickly and could spend all winter
away if we wanted to." They went through the brochures and
decided that a good way to start would be to take a cruise in
the Caribbean. They would think about it anyhow and make a
decision later on.

In this time of moderate prosperity most of those with
steady jobs got holidays, many of them to enjoy the sun in the
winter time. Phoenix and Miami were favorite places to go.
Others went to California and overseas tours were becoming
popular. Airfares were reasonable.

Tom and Susan planned a trip to Hawaii. Tom now got
three weeks holiday and he and Susan loved the sun. They both
had snorkel equipment and took many underwater pictures.

Jim's welding business was doing very well. He now had
three welding rigs and the shop. Peggy had full time work
in the Carebrook Hospital. They had now been married for
five years and decided that it was about time to start a family.
One night Jim came home from work and Peggy said to him,
"Guess what! It won't be long before I have to take some time
off." "Oh," he replied. Are you getting tired of working?" She
said, "Not exactly. In fact my work will be just begun because
we are going to have an addition to our family. Jim beamed
and he gave her a big hug. He said, "How long do we have to
wait?" "Well, I saw the doctor today and he says that it will be
seven months from now." Jim was so excited that he couldn't
sit still. He would have to fix the spare room and get some
baby furniture. Peggy said, "Now hold on Jim. We don't know
if it will be a boy or a girl and we have to get the right colors.

You wouldn't want a boy in a girl's room would you?"

"OK Peggy you are right as usual. It is going to be such a delight to have a little one running around the house." Peggy laughed and replied, "You know Jim there is a lot of TLC has to happen before we hear that pitter patter across the floor. Babies wake up in the night and want to be fed. They have to be changed and burped and they are fussy when their teeth start coming in. You will have to do your share." Jim thought for a minute and said, "Of course I will help you but you will be the food supply for a while." The happy couple had their supper and settled down to watch TV. Peggy noticed that Jim was not paying much attention to the show and a smile kept crossing his face. Little did he know just how much change a baby would make in their home!

Peggy wanted to be a stay-at-home mom and raise their child properly. She didn't want the hassle of getting a baby sitter or putting the child in a day-care. Her mother had stayed home until Peggy was in her teens. Her parents were very good to her and she loved them dearly. These are the people that are most likely to be the most successful parents.

When Sally got the word of having another grandchild she was ecstatic. She had begun to wonder if Jim would ever have a family. Sally was getting on in years and starting to show it. She had put on quite a few extra pounds and, although she and Jim worked out at the health center, she seemed to be slowing down. She was still the main spring at the club house and was forever doing something at the Church. Dave often tried to get her to slow down but he knew there was no stopping her. One day she was coming down the Church steps and tripped and fell. Dave saw that she was hurt and called for an ambulance to take her to the hospital. The X-ray showed cracked vertebrae. This would certainly slow Sally down. She would be in a cast for a few weeks and then she would have to take it easy. Dave had to roll up his sleeves and wait on her and do the cooking and the other housework. Dave did a fine job for the first week but in the second week a housekeeper showed up at the house and Dave was free to take in the odd game of golf. He still spent many hours helping Sally as she regained her mobility and got her strength back again. There were many trips to the therapist but it wasn't long before Sally was walking with the help of a cane. She was a very determined lady and she gained almost complete recovery much faster than her doctor had predicted. Her old friend Tom Epston often called in to see how she was doing. He wouldn't hear of her trying to do any work in the flower beds. That was his job and he made sure there were fresh flowers for the house every day. Dave and Sally were soon on their regular walking routine, even though they didn't go as far as before the accident. Their dog was always with them on the walks or in the car. He seemed to know that Sally was hurting and never left her side. He was such a comfort for her.

By now Dave was showing his age. What hair he had left on his head was almost all white. He still sported his moustache. He held his posture straight and looked quite the gentleman as he walked down the street. His paintings had become quite popular in the galleries and fetched close to $1,000.00 at the showings. He was well known in the art crowd. Sally's pictures also drew a fair price and she was doing more animal portraits now. They had taken to making their own frames now and often people came in to get frames made or having old ones restored. Their art studio was getting to be quite cluttered and Sally persuaded Dave to give up some of the home work. They could do very well just going to art shows without people coming and going to the house. If they were to continue this type of work it would make sense to have a shop in town. Neither of them wanted to get into this because it would mean going to work every day. After all they were supposed to be retired.

Peggy called one day and told Sally that the doctor told her to expect to be going to the hospital any day now. Sally said, "Just let me know and I will be with you." Peggy replied, "You just take it easy. I will be OK. You have to look after yourself. If Jim isn't home maybe Dave could drive me or there are taxis you know." Two nights later Jackie stirred Jim and said, "It is time to go Jim." He very nearly started out without putting on his trousers. They got to the hospital in plenty of time and as the sun was rising over the Monashee Mountains a little girl came forth. Peggy had already chosen a name. "We will call her Betty Anne," she said. That was OK with Jim and he could hardly wait to call Grandma Sally with the good news.

Chapter Seventeen

As it turned out Jim did make a huge shift in his domestic life. Some days he didn't go in to the shop at all. He stayed home and helped Peggy with the children and his whole life seemed to take on a new meaning. The business continued to prosper and his office staff was well trained to handle all of the routine stuff and would only call Jim at home for special instructions.

Jim and Peggy did go to the lake cottage with the two little ones and really enjoyed the peace and tranquility of the place. They returned to their home with renewed ambition and looked forward to do some traveling as soon as the children were old enough. Sally was ever ready to take care of the children and, even at her age, she made a pretty good nanny. As ever, Tom and Susan were ready to help out if she needed anything.

The winter of 1998 was a very mild one. There was very little snow and a serious shortage of water was predicted. Along with it there was a threat of forest fires. Spring came early and turned into a very hot summer. Residents of Carebrook had their water rationed and could water their lawns only twice a week. Those who were caught cheating could have their water supply cut off. Tom's office was busy taking calls and enquiries from orchardists about how to cope with the situation. There were indeed many forest fires reported from all over the Province and fire fighters were brought in from Alberta to help out.

The last week in July brought a weather system from the Pacific and down came the rain. It came in torrents, washing out roads and alarming the fruit growers that their crops would be ruined. At the end of July the Okanagan sun returned and another bounteous crop was harvested. The cherries were harvested just before the rain came so they were saved from spoilage.. The packing house was working to capacity and everybody showed it in their faces. This turned out to be a better than average year in Carebrook.

That winter Jim and Peggy got away for two weeks in Hawaii and came home well tanned and happy as larks. When they went to pick up the children they were met by a not-so-happy Sally. Both children had the measles and had been pretty sick. Sally assured them that they would be OK in a few days. This was just a part of raising kids.

The next couple of years were normal in Carebrook. The children were growing up and going to school and some of them were even old enough to start dating and doing things that teen-agers do. Carebrook was fairly free of vandalism because there was a lot for kids to do and they were brought up by caring parents. There was little tolerance for misbehavior in the schools. The police had an easy time of it in this town. It was considered to be a very friendly place to live. The people welcomed new-comers and made sure that they got involved in community events.

Sally and Dave continued their volunteer work and introduced new programs at the club house. Dave started up a course in public speaking. His students were expected to make public announcements. New-comers were encouraged to introduce themselves and give a brief account ot their life before coming to Carebrook. Some were quite shy about it but were soon part of the crowd. Sally got some of the ladies interested in painting. The young people had the use of the club house for their special events. There was one rule that all had to heed and that was to leave the hall nice and clean as they found it. Any variance from that and they had Aunt Sally to answer to.

Sally was now in her late sixties and starting to show her age. As time went on she seemed to be losing some of her spark. Dave pleaded with her to get a medical assessment but she kept delaying it saying, "Don't fuss over me. I am all right." However, one night she woke Dave and told him that she had a terrible headache and her face felt numb. He got her up immediately and said, "You are going to the hospital right now and I won't take no for an answer." As soon as the doctor saw her he told Dave, "I am admitting her. We will treat her for pain but I think she may have had a stroke." By now she could get no movement on her left side. "Is she going to be alright?" asked Dave. Dr. Smith said that they could probably bring her through this one because it was caught in good time.

Sally remained in the hospital for two months. With the help of therapy she was able to get around in a wheelchair and was soon trying out her legs with the help of a walker. Her speech was slurred for the first three weeks but gradually improved. There was no shortage of visitors coming in to see her. Dave and other family members were there every day. Tom Epston was a frequent visitor. He found it very hard to see his Sally in this state.

Dave took over the running of the house but didn't have to prepare many meals. Susan was for ever bringing stuff over for Dave and staying to clean house and do laundry. Tom kept the lawn and the flower bed in tip-top shape. There were fresh flowers for Sally every day. At last Sally was able to come home but it would be a long recovery time. She couldn't drive the car and she found it very frustrating when the left hand couldn't grasp things very well. In due time, with therapy she improved and was able to do more. One day she asked Dave, "Do you think I could try driving the car?" He replied," Well, we could try a short drive and see how you make out." She had a little difficulty on turns but soon got the hang of it again. They decided that she could drive as long as someone was with her. Tom often came over and went along with her. After about three weeks she was able to navigate on her own. The doctor advised her to use a cane when walking outside or in the shopping center.

Sally was missed at the clubhouse but Shelly and Susan fell into the work and did an admiral job at keeping things going. When Sally finally went to the clubhouse she was surprised by a huge "welcome home" for her put on by the community.

Doctor Smith kept a close watch on Sally and gave Dave instructions on all her needs, i.e. make sure she took her medication and did her exercises. In the meantime Dave had become a pretty good cook. He got to enjoy trying out different recipes, always trying to surprise her and treat her to some pretty fancy dishes.

Sally continued to improve but there were some things that just didn't seem to work for her. For instance, she had trouble reaching up into kitchen cupboards. She seemed to get tired very easily and needed more than her usual eight hours of sleep. Dave tried to tell her that it really didn't matter but how does one convince such an active person.

Dave was showing his age too and was definitely slowing down. Unlike many men of his age, he had put on a bit of weight. With all the anxiety of the past few months his hair showed much grayer. The two of them were the seniors of the family now and enjoying the "golden years."

Jim Bette was now a prominent member of the society and it was he that the younger ones came for advice. He was a successful business man and had inherited many of his mother's attributes in the community. In the upcoming civic election Jim was asked to run for mayor of Carebrook. Peggy encouraged him to take on the challenge. She knew he would do a good job of whatever he undertook. The first thing he knew he was nominated and had been accepted. There was a three-way race for the position and it looked like there would be strong competition. Of course the whole family was out there to help him in his campaign. Finally voting day came and there was a heavy turnout at the polls. The family got together in the clubhouse to watch the results come in. It was a very close race. First Jim was ahead and then he was second. When the final votes were counted the new

Mayor of Carebrook was Jim Bette. The victory party went well past midnight. This was one night that Sally didn't get a full night's sleep.

This was certainly a new pair of shoes for Jim and as he took the chair for his first council meeting he was a little nervous but soon got over that as the many issues came up for debate. He was used to making all the decisions of his business and now others were involved. The big issue of the day was obtaining a new location for the city's waste disposal. Nobody wanted it near their area and of course it could not interfere with the city water source. Tom Epston was the local authority on that and was frequently called to council for environmental issues. There was a basin of land about twenty kilometers north of the lake that seemed to be ideal. There would be some run-off in the spring but it wouldn't take much to divert it away from the site. It was an isolated location and after much debate Carebrook had a new dump.

The tax rate was always a big concern for the residents and a very careful look at the city finances was necessary. Everybody wanted better roads and more recreational facilities. The issue of the Performing Arts Center came to the fore again. It was a controversial issue that was finally to be settled by plebiscite. Jim was fully in favor of it and wasn't backward about voicing his opinion. There were other issues as well that would eventually be voted upon in the fall.

Carebrook now had a population of just over twenty thousand people and was expanding every year. There was a strong move to keep the valley floor for agriculture so new developments were opening up on the higher ground. On the south side of Carebrook the landscape rose gently to five hundred feet above the town site so there was still plenty of room for expansion. This, of course, stirred up a din from those who wanted to save the trees. This again brought Tom Epston into the debate. There was finally a decision made to leave some of the treed areas as park land and development permits were issued. Some of the area had to be taken into the city which was passed without too much to-do.

By now Bobby had earned his papers as a master welder and was able to take over when Jim was not there. In fact Jim made him his senior staff officer and he was well paid with many company perks, including a company car. Jackie was pretty proud of her son. Bobby also loved the country life and spent many hours riding at the farm.

Chapter Eighteen

The Royal Canadian Legion was a very popular place in the city of Carebrook. By now there were only two WW1 veterans left. They were both over one hundred years old and only came to the branch on special occasions, such as Remembrance Day. The long parades on that day had been abandoned in favor of holding the ceremony indoors in the sports center. No more standing out in the cold!

The WW2 veterans were showing their age as well. By now most of them were over eighty years old. The Korean Vets. And returning Peace keepers were becoming the majority and filling positions on the executive.

In earlier times the Legion was considered to be just a drinking hole. The fact of the matter is that by now the Legion gained a lot of respect through their efforts in support of community programs, ie. Financial support for the hospital, the cancer fund, the stroke foundation, and many others. All money gained from gaming enterprises such as Bingo, Keno, and meat draws had to be given away to charitable organizations. Thus the popular belief was that the Legion had loads of money. This was not the case, in fact in later years the Legion had a struggle to keep the branch going.

There were now three care centers for seniors in Carebrook and the Legion organized a committee to visit the veterans in these care facilities on a regular basis. One of the members formed a committee to take these veterans out for an afternoon to various places of entertainment. They organized a sing-song at the Legion once a month. A care-giver accompanied them and waited on them. These fellows could buy a drink and enjoy snacks provided by the Legion. The committee even had a pontoon boat to take them out on the lake if the weather permitted. A couple of them could handle a fishing rod and a few Kokanee were taken back for their cooks to prepare for supper. At Christmas time the Legion treated them with a tray of goodies. The veterans looked forward to these visits. Sometimes the residents wanted information from Veteran Affairs and appointments were set up by the visiting committee. It is for certain that these people would sooner be at home but when they needed more care than could be provided there it was a God-send to have these care facilities where their medication could be monitored as well as a great relief to the spouse at home. Fortunately Sally was able to stay in her own home for now. Dave cared for her and she wanted for nothing. She was still able to get around on her own and of course she had all the family support anybody could wish for. She was in her eighties now and still kept herself prim and proper. She even did some painting and still showed up at the clubhouse for special gatherings. Tom and Susan continued to drop in to see her and of course Tom looked after her lawn and flowers. One thing had changed; she was now "Grandma Sally" rather than "Aunt Sally". The children of the neighborhood treated her with great respect. She always spoke to them with her gentle smile and often had a treat for them. When people showed concern for her health she would say, "What are you worrying about me for? I am as fit as a fiddle." The truth of the matter she was. She had regular visits to her Doctor and had to take a few pills but that was quite normal for a person of her age.

Yes, Sally was an amazing lady. It was not uncommon to see young teen girls coming to her for advice. She had all the answers to the common questions asked by these youngsters ... questions that never seemed to get answered at home. They had plenty of answers offered by their peers but Sally seemed to be able to get the girls on the right track. They trusted her and in most cases took her advice.

There was a drop-in center for teens not far from Sally's house and she often strolled down there to visit these young ones ... mostly teens. There was a young girl, Vera, – age 13 who had run away to Vancouver and got taken in by a pimp. This was a tragic situation, particularly because her family had no idea where she was. The Police were notified but there was no trace of her around Carebrook. Was this another abduction case? The girl's father had a hunch and he took time off from work and went to Vancouver. He scoured the streets in search of his daughter. On the fourth night he thought he saw her get into a car. They were gone before he could get near the spot. He hung around there all the next day and finally he saw her come out of a scruffy rooming house. This time he caught up to her and, with the help of a policeman he got her down to the police station. She was questioned by a very sympathetic police woman. She got the girl calmed down and gave her a decent meal. The next morning she was all cleaned up and agreed to go home with her father. She would have to be under the care of social services and could go home when she showed enough responsibility to abide by house rules and go back to school. She had a caring family but somewhere along the way something had gone wrong. Sally took an interest in Vera and visited the home where she was staying. They had long talks and finally Sally found out what was bothering the girl.

At school one of the boys called her an ugly slut. She had hoped that he found her attractive and would ask her for a date. Heart broken she became despondent and started looking at herself in the mirror until she really believed that she was ugly.

This can be very traumatic for a girl of this age. Soon she thought that everybody was staring at her. She even thought her parents were against her so she decided to run away to Vancouver. A young girl in this state is easy prey for a pimp.

Sally convinced her that she was indeed a very attractive young lady and invited her to her house. It wasn't long before she was laughing and was well on the way back to normal. Soon after she was allowed to move back with her family and she went on to finish high school. Sally seemed to have this magic in her that could boost the self-esteem in anyone.

About this time Sally was starting to feel that couldn't do the things she used to do. Dave told her, "You know Sally, we can easily afford to hire somebody to come in and do the house cleaning and help with the washing and ironing." Sally insisted that she could carry on for now but Dave kept on with it until Sally consented to place an ad. in the paper. There were a number of responses but Sally just couldn't seem to find someone suitable. A few weeks later there was a knock at the door. It was Vera, the girl Sally had recently helped out of a bit of a social problem. Sally invited her in and asked her how things were going. Vera answered, "I am back in school and doing just fine. I need a job to save up for college and saw your ad. in the paper. Sally gasped, "Are you asking me for a job Vera?" Vera replied, "I would like to work here part time and I know we would get along fine." Sally sensed that Vera was sincere and she would probably be a good worker so she said, "I will let you start as soon as you can but it will only be part – time because I don't want it to interfere with your school work." So it came to be that Vera became a valued member of the family. She was very attentive to Sally's wishes and didn't hesitate to do many extra things, like run errands, and didn't expect to be paid extra. Dave was overjoyed to see Sally taking it a bit easier. He took a great interest in Vera's school work and often coached her through difficult problems.

As Vera was nearing her graduation from high school she was thinking about her future career. She talked to Sally and Dave many times and one day she announced that she would like to take training in nursing, specializing in looking after the aged in care homes. After all she had the experience of looking after Sally. Sally and Dave both warned her that she would likely run into much more difficult situations than at their house. Vera was determined and she registered at the college for the fall semester.

Chapter Ninteen

During the next couple of years Sally started feeling the effects of arthritis and started using a cane when she went walking, Dave went with her and helped her when she needed it. When the snow came she pretty much stayed indoors. She had a dreadful fear of slipping on the ice. Vera was a great help to her when it came to bathing and getting in and out of her clothes.

Sally's family kept a close watch on her and Tom still looked after the grounds. Dave was getting on in years as well but was in good health and was still able to drive the car. They were usually able to go to Church on Sunday and occasionally took in a performance at the performing arts center.

Sally was very satisfied that all her family was doing well. They lived in harmony and still had their gatherings at the club house. This facility had been renovated and enlarged a number of times over the years. It was a focal point in the community where many family celebrations were held. Carebrook, now a city, was still a peaceful place to live. The crime rate was well below average and it had now become a destination for tourists. A ski hill had been developed, complete with chair lifts and a fine clubhouse at the top. There were now two added camp grounds on the lake and fishing for kokanee was a great attraction. Land had been reserved on the south side of town and two professional class golf courses had been developed. The economy of the area was doing well and most of the people were thriving in Carebrook.

One morning Dave was startled from his sleep by a thump. Sally had fallen out of bed and was lying on the floor. Dave called Vera and told her to call 911 for an ambulance. They managed to get Sally on to the bed. It was obvious that she had another stroke. This time her whole left side seemed to be paralyzed. The ambulance arrived and Sally was off to the hospital. Surely enough, it was a stroke and she would have to remain in hospital for some time.

After a few days Sally was able to have visitors. Her room was soon decorated with cards and flowers. Tom and Susan brought her up a bouquet of lilacs from her favorite bush that had been planted so many years ago by Tom. All her family rallied around and visited her on a regular basis. The doctor said that it was unlikely that she would walk again. This meant that Sally would now be confined to a wheel chair.

The realization of this was a blow to her but she was determined to make the most of it so long as she could return to her beloved home. She still had her cheery smile and, although her speech was slurred, she always said, "Oh! I'm alright. Stop worrying about me."

Sally learned to maneuver the wheel chair quite quickly and was up and down the hospital hallways in no time. The nurses threatened to put a bell on her so they could keep track of her. And guess what she was up to in much of her time. She was talking to other patients and cheering them up. The doctors and nurses often said, "That is the best therapy for the likes of a girl like Sally," Everybody on the third floor knew her and looked forward to her visits.

One morning the doctor came in and said to her, "I

think you can go home tomorrow. I know you have lots of family support and the district nurse will be calling on you." Even though Sally was overjoyed with the good news, she said to the nurse, I'm going to miss this place and all the good friends I have made."

So it was that Dave and Shelly arrived at the hospital and took Sally home. Her left arm and hand were almost useless but she was soon a master of that wheelchair and was trekking around the house in grand style. She was a little dubious about letting Dave loose in her kitchen but, after all, he had been managing for the months she had been in the hospital. Daily he surprised her with new dishes he had found in her recipe books. He said, "You know Sally, I rather enjoy cooking. It is much like creating a new picture in my art studio."

Tom and Susan were frequent visitors. Tom had been such a close friend for so many years and his family was considered as part of Sally's family. The great-grand children were delighted when they were told they were going over to see Grandma Sally.

Gradually Sally gained a little more use of her left hand and one day she said to Dave, "You know Dave; I think that I will try to take a few steps." "Oh no you don't!" he replied. "Not without the help of your therapist." She kept working her legs and feet as she sat in her chair and the next time Sue, her therapist, was there, Sally said to her, "Do you suppose I could try standing up on my own two feet?" Sue asked, "Do you really think you could do it?" Sally said, "Let's give it a try." She called Vera to be on hand to help out and they managed to get Sally to a very shaky stand. She even put one foot ahead of the other in an attempt to take a step. Sue said, "Not so fast Sally you must learn to stand with support and don't you dare try to do it on your own. We will get a little strength in those legs of yours and then we will set up parallel bars for and you are going to have to understand that it is going to take a long time before you can walk on your own." Indeed the process was slow but Sally was determined and it wasn't long before she could stand and hang on to the bed. Dave and Vera saw to it that she didn't try to do it on her own. One day they got her over to the parallel bars and she was actually able to take a couple of steps. Sally proclaimed, "I am going to be walking within a month; just you wait and see."

After about a month Sue came to the house with a pair of crutches. Sally glared at them and said, "I won't be using those things for very long. Let's get on with the lesson." With a great deal of perseverance Sally was soon shuffling around on the crutches. She hated them and snorted, "One would think I was a cripple or something!"

As the summer passed into fall Sally became surer of herself and tried walking with a cane. Dave was very wary about it and wouldn't let her do it on her own. By Christmas time Sally was getting around quite well with the cane. She was able to join all the family at the clubhouse for a grand Christmas party. Everybody welcomed her back and fussed over her. She didn't care about the fussing but had a wonderful time. When she got home she was exhausted and sank into her bed for a deep and satisfied sleep. Dave was so proud of her. After all, the first prognosis was that the best she could expect was to spend the rest of her days in a wheel chair.

One day in April Tom was over cleaning up the flower gardens and raking the lawn. When he was finished he came into the house and sat down for a cup of tea with Sally and Dave. Sally said, "You know Tom, it will be sixty years ago next week that we met by the creek. Do you still remember that day Tom?" "Of course I do," replied Tom. "I was just a kid then but look at all the good times we have had since then. Sally said, "I don't remember the exact date but I would like you to take me there, the exact spot, for old times sake. Let's make it some time next week. Pick a day when the sun is shining. I know there is a burm there now but there is a path further up and we can go that way so I won't have to climb the burm. It was all set and Tom would pick the day. It had been an early spring and all the ice was gone from the lake. The birds had returned to their nesting spots and of course all the water creatures would be visible.

On a Wednesday morning Tom phoned Sally and said "I think this would be a grand day to take you to the creek." Sally screamed, "Oh

Tom' it does look just like the day I met you. I will be waiting for you and it must be just you and I." A half hour later Tom was there and got Sally into the car and they were on their way. They stopped at the trail cut off and walked slowly to the spot where they had met. Sally gazed into the water and exclaimed, "Look at the minnows Tom; they are still here." Tom suggested that they must be quite a few generations later than the ones you saw on that day." Sally said, "Look at the red-wing blackbirds on those rushes over there and there is a heron over there as well."

As they stood there they were disturbed by the barking of a dog. A young lad came running up and shouted out, "Hi grandpa and hi Grandma Sally!" Sally said, "That is a nice dog you have. What is his name? The young lad [about ten years old] said, "His name is Ruff. He is a good dog and he won't bite you. Would you like to pet him?"

This made Sally's day. The three of them and Ruff went back to the car and drove down the *lane* to Tom's house which still held the name of the house at the end of the lane. After a nice cup of tea with Tom and Susan, Tom took Sally back home. This had been one of the most memorable days of her life. She wiped a tear from her eyes as she bid Tom farewell and thanked him for such a wonderful experience. This was the last time Sally was to visit this spot but it was ever dear to her.

From this time on Sally became frailer and didn't get out very often. Dave and Sally lived on in their comfortable home and with Vera there to help her she didn't even have to have the district nurse call around. After all Vera was fully qualified to look after the elderly.

Sally and Dave often sat by the fire and talked about days gone by. They both agreed that life had been good to them. Occasionally young girls would still drop in to talk to Sally. She was a grand old lady and still had great concerns for the young ones.

Late one night that winter Dave was wakened by a strange noise. Sally was breathing very heavily and there was a nasty wheeze with it. She had a pain in her chest and she suggested that perhaps Dave should call the ambulance and get her to the hospital. When she got to emergency the doctor examined her and told Dave that he should notify the family.

The next evening all the family was around her as she breathed her last breath. Sally had passed on to her heavenly father. The community was grieved to hear of the passing of this wonderful lady who had played such a significant part in so many lives in the city of Carebrook. The funereal service was moved to the auditorium because the Church would not be large enough to hold the expected crowd. Indeed people came from far and wide and the hall was filled with flowers. As could be expected Tom Epston made sure there was a large bouquet of lilacs placed on the alter. Though she was cremated a memorial stone was placed in the cemetery in her honor.

Her epitaph read:

SALLY N. FROST
1918-2000
LOVED BY ALL
WHO KNEW HER

She had left a request to have her ashes sprinkled in the lake near where the brook entered. This was done in a private ceremony by her beloved family a month later.

This story marks the history of over eighty years of a growing town in one of the most picturesque valleys in the province of British Columbia.

ISBN 142512346-5

9 781425 123468